ONCE A LEGEND

ONCE A LEGEND

Jack Cummings

Walker and Company
New York

First published in the United States of America in 1988 by the Walker Publishing Company, Inc.

Published simultaneously in Canada by Thomas Allen & Son Canada, Limited, Markham, Ontario.

Library of Congress Cataloging-in-Publication Data

Cummings, Jack, 1925–
    Once a legend / Jack Cummings.
        p.   cm.
    ISBN 0-8027-4075-8
    I. Title.
PS3553.U44405   1988   813′.54—dc19   87-17307

Printed in the United States of America

10 9 8 7 6 5 4 3 2 1

Frank Ladd was once a legend in the Old West. Now he had a second chance.

CHAPTER 1

I RODE into Staffold, Arizona, in the summer of 1915, and my first thought was that it wasn't much of a town to end up in, for a man who'd been as big a Western legend as Frank Ladd.

And then I thought, what the hell, it had been twenty years since Ladd brought in Ike Tolbert alive after Tolbert swore he'd kill any lawman that hunted him down.

And a lot of things changed, in twenty years, one of them being that I was now a twenty-five-year-old drifter and some-time cowhand in a West that was almost gone.

Which was why I'd come to Staffold. I'd heard that Ladd lately was working in Morency's Saloon & Gambling as a part-time attraction and greeter, and I was of a mind to shake the hand of the man who had been my boyhood hero.

I tied my horse to the hitchrack and glanced at the new Studebaker automobile parked across the paved main street. The sight of it made me grit my teeth. I'm one of those people who leans toward nostalgia, I guess. I relished the events I'd heard about in my kid days. Events I'd never get a chance to experience during my own adult lifetime.

He was there, just as I expected him to be, only older of course. Looked much older than I'd thought he would.

He was giving the gladhand to a couple of well-dressed men, tourists by their looks, and I had the feeling they'd just arrived in town in that shiny phaeton outside.

The barman was looking on approvingly. He could have been Morency himself.

Ladd stood tall for his fifty years, still a fine-physiqued man carrying very little fat and impressive as hell with a

1

fancy ivory-handled Colt Peacemaker slung low on his right thigh.

He was wearing black. Shirt, belt, holster, trousers, and boots. His hair was iron gray and cut short, and his features were darkened by the years he'd spent under the Arizona sun. He was handsome in a craggy sort of way. Wherever his hat was, I'd have bet it was black too.

When I pushed into the saloon, he was the first to look my way. I got the impression he made his appraisal instinctively, almost without thought, and I was dismissed—although I imagined he gave me the slightest of nods before turning back to his business of being a celebrity for the tourists.

I steered to the bar, ordered a whiskey and waited my chance. He had a drink with two patrons, then he left them at a table with a bottle between them and went to mingling with the others.

The place was crowded, it being a Saturday afternoon, and I began to wish I'd come another time. Still, it gave me a chance to study him, and I guess a lot of what I'd felt as a kid came back to me, because I kept thinking: a fine old man, a *fine* old man.

Once or twice he looked my way as he surveyed the crowd. I suppose he owed his having lived this long to taking the precaution of being always on guard for rep-hungry lunatics or old enemies who might take their chance, especially now that he was way past his prime.

The thought struck me then that maybe those glances he gave me were due to this, and for one crazy minute I swelled with a kind of pride that he'd be considering me a threat.

And then I turned cold with another thought. Suppose he *did* consider me dangerous? I began to wish to hell I hadn't strapped on the old Smith & Wesson I usually carried in my saddlebag. I'd had a lot of practice shooting with it, just because I enjoyed it and was good at it. But the day of the gunfighter was over, and I had no ambitions along those lines.

I was still thinking this over when he came toward me. My blood ran colder, but I wasn't really scared. Crazy or not, something came over me: that wild, desperate feeling a man making a play against his kind gets.

Still, it was a relief when he pushed to the bar beside me, smiled, and said, "How're you doing, boy?"

"Mr. Ladd?" I said.

"Right, boy."

I shoved out my hand. "I've been a longtime admirer of yours, sir."

He took my hand and his grip was firm, but he quickly let go. No man was going to hang onto Frank Ladd's gunhand very long, I thought.

"Can I buy you a drink, sir?"

He gave me a close look and said, "Lord, no, boy!" He paused then, as if he thought I might be offended. "I appreciate the offer, but save your money. I have to accept more than enough drinks when I'm entertaining."

"Entertaining?"

"Hell, what else would you call it? I'm here to entertain Morency's customers. Sort of like a performing bear. All I have to do is stand on my hind legs and walk around—and shake hands." His face took on a certain bitter look. "Ain't much different from what a trained bear does at that, except a bear has to be taught these things. To me, nowadays anyhow, it comes right natural."

I didn't want to say the wrong thing, so I kept my mouth shut.

"It may look easy to do, boy," he said. "But it ain't. Not really."

"Why do you do it then, sir?"

"That's a big question. But the big answer is there ain't much use for my talents nowadays."

"As a manhunter, you mean?"

"You could say that."

"You were—are—very famous, sir," I said.

"Yeah," he said, looking into the mirror behind the bar to watch the crowd behind us. "That's what brings the customers in. Wasn't for that, I'd likely be swamping out the place instead of strutting around in these fancy circus duds with a ivory-handled show pistol."

"Seems to me that what you do ought to make you feel proud," I said.

"Well, it don't, boy. It surely don't. But it's a bare living, and I got to do something to buy the groceries. I got a young wife, boy."

"Is that a fact, sir?"

He grinned. "Well, not quite as young as you, I reckon. Holds her age well, though, for thirty-five." He paused. "I shouldn't have said that, boy, I surely shouldn't. Women don't like their age to be known. Especially if they carry their good looks well."

I was a little surprised that he was married. I'd just never thought about it. A man like the famous Frank Ladd, it somehow just seemed proper that he'd be a lifelong bachelor.

"Yep," he said. "Been married to her for fifteen years now." He seemed to be giving that fact some thought, then said suddenly, "Say, I might take you up on that drink, after all."

I realized then that he was carrying a fair-sized load already, like maybe he'd shared more than a few with those he was hired to greet. I signaled the bartender, and he came down to us and pushed out a drink to Ladd and gave me a refill when I nodded. I laid down a coin to pay for them.

"Thanks, boy," Frank Ladd said.

"My pleasure, sir." I hesitated, then said, "What does your wife think of you working here?"

"Well, she wouldn't stand for it, if I was swamping," he said. "But me working as a celebrity, she can live with that, even though the pay is poor." He paused. "Goddammit, boy! You got to remember she was still a girl when she met me, and I was sheriff over to Pinto County at the time and riding high on a reputation, and I reckon she was pretty much bamboozled by it all. I was at my peak right about then, and well, hell, things never got better from then on, financially or otherwise, but they did get some worse. All that wears away at a woman, I reckon, more than it does a man."

"You still got your fame, Mr. Ladd. That's what brought me across half the Territory—I mean the state—to meet you."

I'd recalled that Arizona had been a state now for over three years.

"Yeah, I still got that, or leastwise some of it," he said.

"Well, boy—what was your name again?"

"Hardin, sir. Drew Hardin."

He looked a shade startled. "Any kin to John Wesley Hardin?"

"No, sir! None at all." John Wesley Hardin, now dead, had been the Texas gunfighter who killed forty-some men. I'd had the question put to me before, and as far as I had ever found out our family had no connection with his.

"Glad to hear that, boy, glad to hear that," Frank Ladd said. "He was a vicious dog who should have been killed when he was a pup." He paused. "Well, thanks for the drink, Drew, and now I'd best mix with these other paying guests. I see old Morency starting to fidget because I'm not drumming up trade. I'll maybe see you around, if you stay a while in Staffold."

I could see no reason then that I'd be hanging around, since Staffold was mostly a mining town, but I wanted to be polite and I said, "That'd be my pleasure, Mr. Ladd."

He nodded and moved away.

Well, it was strange how things worked out. I mean the way everything seemed to fall into place after I met him.

For me, and for him.

And for that young wife of his too.

CHAPTER 2

IT all began when they finally released Ike Tolbert out of the state prison at Florence, after him doing twenty years, the first fourteen of it at Yuma Territorial.

You might have thought that all those years in those hellholes would have taught the old outlaw that crime did not pay.

But it didn't.

Because Ike hadn't been out more than two weeks when he hunted down the judge who'd given him that stiff sentence.

He found him asleep in his bachelor bungalow on the outskirts of Tucson. He filled him full of .45 slugs from a revolver of unknown make and then cut off his head and stuck it on a point of the whitewashed picket gate out front.

An attorney, making a professional call on the retired judge, was the first to meet the head face to face as he opened the gate, and he dropped dead of a heart attack.

Some children playing down the road noticed this and investigated and spread an alarm. It wasn't long before the authorities knew they'd made a mistake in letting Tolbert out.

And it wasn't long before word got to Frank Ladd. It got to him late the same day that I'd met him in Morency's Saloon.

I went back to Morency's after sleeping out under the stars that night. I figured the polite thing was to say goodbye to Ladd before I drifted on.

It was just after the saloon opened, and it was empty except for Morency, who was behind his bar straightening up things

6

like most barmen do when they don't have any customers to deal with.

I asked what hours Ladd came on shift, although I knew it was only a part-time job.

"Peak hours only," Morency said. "I can't afford to pay him to hang around when there ain't any business to be had."

"And when would that be?"

"Some afternoons, evenings," Morency said. He was a fat man with a red face, and he had an expression that wasn't near as happy as it had been the day before.

"Thanks," I said and turned away.

"He won't be in today at all," the bar owner said.

That stopped me, and I turned back.

"He sent word earlier to tell me that," Morency said.

"How come?"

"They've released Ike Tolbert."

It took a minute for that to sink in. "Ike Tolbert?" I asked. "You mean the old outlaw that made Mr. Ladd famous?"

"Yeah."

"So what's that got to do with Mr. Ladd now?"

"How the hell do I know what's going through the old bastard's head?" Morency said.

That made me mad. "You hadn't ought to speak disrespectful of Mr. Ladd like that!"

"Why not?" Morency said, and I could tell he was pretty sore or he wouldn't have said what he said next, not when he counted on Ladd to draw the crowds. He said, "The old bastard is a has-been, and been that way for years. He wouldn't be working in a saloon if he wasn't."

"Mr. Ladd was a great Western lawman," I said. I was shocked to hear anybody talk about Ladd that way.

"*Was*, is right. He fit right in, in his day, which was twenty years ago. But, dammit, fella, things have changed. There's new ways of law enforcement now. Crime fighting has become scientific, like that guy over in France who discovered you can tell who somebody is by rubbing ink on his fingers and looking at them, or such like. We got telephones linking a quarter of the towns in the state. And there must be a couple hundred automobiles in Arizona now. These are modern times, son."

"So?" I said.

"Ladd never changed with the times. He had his own set ways of lawdogging, and refused to adopt the new. He stuck to the old, and folks got fed up and he couldn't get reelected over in Pinto County no more. He town-marshaled for awhile, getting by on his reputation. Meanwhile Lola had married him. I reckon she made a mistake there, and she damn well knows it now."

"Lola?" I said.

"His wife. Hell, she's fifteen years younger than him." Morency seemed to realize he was getting loose-mouthed, and he said, "The hell of it is, Frank is smart enough—he just never had the inclination to grow with the times."

"You got anything more to say to me about Mr. Ladd?" I said coldly.

He gave me a close look for the first time, and I could see him grow aware that maybe he was criticizing Frank Ladd to the wrong man.

"No," he said, and began polishing his bar with the towel he grabbed up. "I got nothing to say." He paused, then said, "You kind of caught me in a off moment, fella. I'd appreciate it if you wouldn't mention none of what I said to Frank."

I didn't give him any satisfaction.

"If he's a friend of yours, you wouldn't want to hurt his feelings, would you?" There was a kind of pleading in his voice now, like not many men would want Frank Ladd sore at them.

I knew I wouldn't. I left the place without saying yes or no. Let Morency sweat, I thought.

What he'd said about Ike Tolbert being free, though, that was really something to think about! After all those years of

Tolbert just being a name in the saga of Frank Ladd, here he was on the prod again—real, live, and dangerous.

I think I said before that I'm kind of nostalgic by nature, and having Ike Tolbert suddenly alive in these modern times of 1915 was as if they'd dug up the frozen remains of some old caveman and thawed him out to life.

I still wanted to say goodbye to Ladd, but in my resentment at Morency's comments I'd forgot to ask where he lived. But it didn't take me long to find out from one of the townsmen I met on the street.

He lived on the outskirts, in what was not much more than a miner's shack. Somebody had tried to improve the looks of the place with a small cactus garden out front, there being no chance of keeping flowers alive during the summer. It was a neatly kept garden, like it was done by a woman's hand.

There was an open shed out back with some tack hanging in it, where he could stable a horse. And that was about all. It sure wasn't much of a place for a man like him to have to live in.

There was a front screen door, with a wood door behind it standing open. I went up and knocked. Nobody answered at first, and I kept staring through the screen trying to see if anybody was home. And then I made out the well-formed figure of a woman in a tight-fitting house dress on the other side.

"I'm looking for Mr. Ladd," I said.

"He's not in—just now."

She had a quiet voice. It struck me that there was no fear in it.

While I was thinking about this, she spoke again. "What was it you wanted?"

"I was just leaving town, and I wanted to say goodbye to him."

"Friend of his?"

"Well, not exactly. I only met him yesterday, but I rode

across half of Arizona to meet him. Kind of an admirer, I guess you'd say."

She pushed against the screen door, and I backed up to let it open, and she stepped out.

I didn't back up another step. I just stood there looking at her and thinking what a lucky old man Frank Ladd was to have a young wife with the kind of looks she had.

She let the door's spring slam it shut behind her, and then she smiled. She stared right into my eyes and neither of us spoke for a minute. Then she said, "You're pretty young to be an admirer of Frank's."

"Been so since I was a little kid," I said.

"He had a lot of admirers back about then."

"He's got a lot of them yet," I said, coming to his defense like I'd done with Morency, without even intending to.

Her smile widened, and she had beautiful teeth. "It's nice to hear you say that."

"It's the truth, ma'am."

She just kept smiling at me.

I let my eyes run down over her, and when I looked back up at her face I saw she was doing the same thing to me. When our glances met again, she had stopped smiling and her voice sounded a little husky. "You've got a lean, tough look about you," she said. "Like maybe you've been cowboy-ing."

"Some," I said.

"I don't know when Frank will be back," she said. "I'd invite you in to wait, but the house is a mess. Two people in a place this size, it's kind of hard to keep it in order."

I tried to see in, having a big urge to be in there with her. From what I could make out through the screen the place looked neat as a pin.

I was about to say so, and it seemed like this was what she was waiting for, but then suddenly I thought about Ladd and how big he stood to me, and the thought came that inside that little place was about an acre of dangerous ground.

A little frown puckered her neatly kept eyebrows, then after a minute it went away. She said again, "You *are* pretty young to be an admirer of Frank's. Not a day over thirty, I'll bet."

I should have just nodded, but before I thought I said, "Only twenty-five, ma'am," and I wanted to kick myself for it.

I felt better immediately when she said, "You are very mature-looking for your age."

"I'm glad you think so, ma'am."

"Why?" she said.

She had me there. I only knew it was so.

Then she smiled again, almost as if she was laughing at me, and I don't know what might have happened next if at that moment her smile hadn't left her and she stared down the road so hard I turned to see what she was staring at.

It was Frank Ladd coming toward us. He wasn't walking. He was riding a big buckskin gelding, and he looked different somehow, and when he got closer I saw the fancy black duds were gone. He was wearing rangerider brown pants and a hickory shirt and a gray old Stetson. And he had a worn cartridge belt around his hips instead of the *buscadero* circus rig he'd worn in the saloon. The ivory-handled show pistol had been replaced by one with worn walnut grips.

His wife said, "I knew something was up when he left this morning."

"Like what, ma'am?"

"I don't know."

He rode up close, stared at me like he couldn't quite place me at first. Then he said, "Why hello, boy!" He looked from me to his wife, and just for a minute I thought a strange expression flitted across his face. But I could have been mistaken. Maybe it was just my guilt at the thoughts I'd been having.

He sat there in a well-used saddle and said, "Lola, I want you to meet Drew Hardin. Young fella rode clear across the state just to shake my hand."

"Only half-across, sir," I said. Which shows I was kind of befuddled because of what I'd been thinking a few minutes before. I was damned glad right about then that I'd not gone inside with Lola.

And what do you think he said then? "Go on in, you two. I'll be right in soon as I stable the buckskin," and he rode around in back and left us there alone together.

"You heard him, Drew," she said, using my first name like we were old acquaintances. "No need to be afraid now."

That stung me enough that I said, "I wasn't afraid!"

"Maybe I was mistaken."

"Damned lucky," I said.

She gave a little laugh.

"It wouldn't have been funny," I said.

She stopped laughing, and said, "No, you're right. It *was* lucky. He may be a has-been, but he's no man to trifle with, even now."

"I'm damned sure of that," I said. But I followed her in.

CHAPTER 3

WE just sat and looked at each other, waiting for Frank to come in from unsaddling his horse. I glanced a couple of times around the room, and like I'd thought earlier, the place was clean and well-kept. She was a good housekeeper.

Frank came through the door and there was an air about him that was different from what it had been in Morency's place. He had a vitality now that had been missing then. You could see it in his face. In the way he walked and stood, even.

"I got to tell you," he said right off, talking to both of us, "there's big news happened the last couple of weeks. I just heard late last night when the telegrapher gave me the message." He paused. "I didn't tell you, Lola, because I wanted to make sure this morning. It's true."

She said, sharply, "What is?"

"They released Ike Tolbert."

She kept staring at him, not saying a word.

I said, "I heard, Mr. Ladd. Morency told me an hour or so ago."

He nodded. "Twenty years the poor bastard was locked up because of me. A hell of a sentence for four or five train robberies."

Lola spoke up then. "What's his release got to do with you, Frank? You didn't sentence him."

"No," Ladd said. "I didn't."

"You shouldn't have anything to worry about, then," she said.

"Hell, I ain't worried, Lola. I ain't figuring on him coming after me. I'm figuring on going after him."

13

She gave him a blank look, then said. "Why, Frank? What for?"

"Hell, he's been out no more than a couple of weeks, and already he's in worse trouble than he was in the old days."

When he said "the old days," something began to stir in my mind.

"How can that be, Frank?" Lola said.

"The poor damned fool went and killed Judge Farrell, the one that gave him that maximum sentence."

"He had his revenge, then."

"He did, and then some. He got the prosecuting attorney, too."

I said, "He must have been pretty busy with his gun."

"He didn't use a gun—on the judge, yes—but the prosecutor dropped dead when he saw Farrell's head stuck on a gatepost."

Lola gave a little scream, and I felt my stomach turn over. I said, stupidly, "Head? Gatepost?"

Ladd gave a grim chuckle and shook his head. Then a thoughtful look came over his face and he said, "Shows what can happen to a man when you shut him up in a hellhole for twenty years."

"Frank!" Lola said. "You can't be sympathizing with him!"

He didn't answer right away, which surprised me.

Finally, he said, "Maybe I do, in a way. I always did think he got a worse sentence than he deserved. Hell, John Wesley Hardin—no relation to this young fella here—only did fifteen in the Texas pen, and he killed more than forty men for not much reason at all. Tolbert's trouble and bad luck was that the powerful railroad interests got an example made of him."

Lola shook her head. "Frank, tell the truth. You've always known that Tolbert was the one who made you a big man. In all the years of our marriage, I've never heard you say a harsh word about him."

He looked at her angrily for a moment, and then the anger

left his face and was overcome by a kind of wondering look, as if he realized for the first time that there was at least some truth in what she said.

She said, "The way you feel about him, why would you consider going after him?"

He gave her a long, cool stare. "Money, Lola. Does that interest you? On account of what he did to the judge, they've put a bounty of five thousand dollars on him, dead or alive."

"Five *thousand!*" she said, and I could see she was interested, all right.

"Five *thousand*, Frank?" she said again.

He was wearing a faint, grim smile as he looked at her. "That's one reason," he said. "And there's the other. I'm sick and tired of being a glorified saloon swamper in a Wild West costume luring in suckers to Morency's bar and gaming tables."

I could see what he meant there, all right. In fact, I was as excited as he was, maybe more, just thinking about him doing a repeat of the act that made him a legend. I began to wonder if there was some way I could be an actual witness to it. It would be like living in the old days. A chance to be a part of a time much different from modern 1915.

Then she said something that made me wonder whether she was genuinely concerned about his welfare or if it was something else. She said, "You're twenty years older now, Frank. Do you think you could do it?"

If she wasn't really concerned, then it was a hell of a cruel thing to say. I looked at him to see how he'd take it. He was poker-faced, so I couldn't tell.

"Are you listening to me, Frank?" she said.

He didn't say anything.

I answered, even though I knew I shouldn't. I said, "Mr. Ladd is just as good a man as he used to be."

She turned to me. "And what would you know about that?"

I could feel my face flushing, because it seemed that maybe she was referring to something more intimate than his ability as a lawman. She kept her eyes on me and I kept flushing. Whatever she meant, it seemed to me that it wasn't a proper thing to be referring to in front of the man himself.

And then she made it worse. She smiled at me, a knowing smile like now we shared a secret about him.

It made me uncomfortable as hell. I had to force myself to look at Ladd. His face was blank.

But he said, "I can do it, Lola. Don't you worry none about me." Just saying it seemed to make him feel better.

"Who telegraphed the news to you?" she said.

"The sheriff over to Tucson. That's where the killing of the judge took place."

"Why you?" she said.

"Hell, he's an old friend of mine, you know that. Was a deputy of mine at one time. He thought I might be interested."

"Five thousand dollars makes it interesting, all right," Lola said. "It's going to make it interesting to some other bounty hunters though, Frank." She paused. "Men who've kept up with the times, know the new methods. Men that know how to drive automobiles, use the newest inventions. The way you've been," she said—and I could sense the resentment in her voice—"you've never got over your love of the past."

How was that for sticking a knife in him? But he didn't flare up when she said it. Instead, he said, "That just might help, Lola. Him and me both being pretty ignorant of all this modern crap. We'd be of a common mind, so to speak."

I couldn't tell if he was joking or not.

"Frank," she said, "you'll never stop living over the old days. You know why that is? It's because you hit your peak back then."

"Maybe, Lola, maybe," he said.

I hated the way she talked to him. But I remembered the Bible saying something about no man being prophet to his own kinfolks, or something like that, and I guess that's the way it gets to be between a man and his wife after the honeymoon is over. Right then I kind of filed it away in my mind to never get married.

But when I looked at her, I could see how easy it would be for a man not to keep a resolution like that. I guess most men get trapped that way. They get to looking and their resolution goes to hell.

Just as if she was reading my thoughts, she turned to me and smiled again. But when she spoke I knew it wasn't that at all.

She said, "Maybe you should take along a young man with you, Frank. Somebody who could remind you of how it is nowadays."

"Dammit, Lola! I know how it is. It's just that I got my own ways of doing things." He paused. "Besides, it ain't fitting for newfangled methods to be used against a man who's been put away as long as Ike was."

"What do you mean, it isn't fitting?"

"What I mean, it ain't fair."

"Are you crazy? Is sticking a man's head on a gatepost fair?"

"I mean," Ladd said, "he ought to be given a sporting chance."

She looked at me and shook her head, kind of like he was a hopeless case. I pretended not to notice this. To be truthful, I was on Ladd's side all the way. I understood exactly what he was saying and how he felt because I felt the same way. It seemed it would be unfair, somehow, to use against Tolbert all the things that had come into being while he was in a cell at Yuma.

Of course, not using them could make the job of catching him a hell of a lot of tougher. But what an achievement that could be, if you could pull it off!

Lola had done one thing for *me*, though. She'd put the bee in his head about taking me along to help him.

Right then he spoke about it. "That pistol you're packing, Drew. You any good with it?"

"Pretty good," I said. "I mean against tin cans and such." I'd put the gun on again just to say goodbye to him, figuring it'd be appropriate, sort of. "I never shot it at a man, though." Then I spoke up real quick. "I could help you make camp and the like, Mr. Ladd. There'd be other ways I might be useful to you on the trail. I've rode considerable back country, roaming around. Of course it all depends on where you'd be going."

He appeared to be considering it, but then he dashed my hopes. "You any good with a rifle? I mean, are you *real* good?"

Well, I wanted to lie so bad I could taste it. But I said no.

"I couldn't pay you anything," he said. "Not at the start. If we got the job done, I'd give you a hundred a month for the time you spent or fraction thereof."

"I'd be glad to accept those terms, sir."

"You can call me Frank," he said.

Looking back, I know now that I should have suspected something when he took me on as a partner so easily. Especially when another peculiar thing happened right after.

"You're going to need me along, too, Frank," Lola said.

I expected him to rare up and call it a ridiculous idea. Who ever heard of taking a woman along on a bounty hunt?

But he didn't react like that at all. Instead he was quiet for a minute, and kind of thoughtful.

"You know that, don't you, Frank?" she said. "This young man here has just told you he's not much use with a rifle."

"What's that got to do with it?" I said.

She said, "Frank?" And she waited for him to answer.

He hesitated a little longer, then said, "The truth is, boy, my eyesight ain't what it used to be when it comes to distance."

I was shocked to hear that. It hadn't occurred to me that there was more reason for him working in a saloon than I thought. But I said, "And with your handgun?"

"I see good as ever at sixgun range," he said. "But if I know Ike, he'll head for that *malpais* country down Pinacate way. You can see where a rifle could come in handy, country like that."

"I still don't understand," I said, looking from him to her.

"Tell him, Frank. It's no secret. Even if, after all these years, nobody remembers."

He cleared his throat like he was going to tell me a long story. "It's Lola," he said. "When I met her, I was the sheriff over to Pinto County like I think I told you." He paused. "There was one of them little Wild West shows come through. This was back in 1900, and Buffalo Bill Cody had been touring with his big show around the nation since '85 and by now he had a bunch of two-bit imitators."

"She was with the show?"

"Yep. And when they hit the county seat at Pinto, they went flat busted, and some of the local creditors forced me to attach the assets for bankruptcy proceedings."

I looked across at Lola and her eyes met mine, and they had a kind of shining look I hadn't seen before. "Tell him, Frank," she said.

"Lola here," he said, "was a crack rifle shot with the show."

"And stranded," she said. She looked at me. "And there was the famous Frank Ladd, taking an interest in me."

"Where'd you learn to shoot?" I said.

"I grew up on a hardscrabble ranch," she said. "I learned to shoot game for our table, so's my pa didn't have to kill off the few head of cattle he ran." She paused. "I can ride too, Drew. Maybe better than you can. You won't find me any trouble on the trail. I know the life well enough."

He said something then that further surprised me: "It won't be the first time. I took her along a few times after I lost out as sheriff and went to bountying." He stopped then suddenly, as if he realized he was maybe talking too much. Then he said, "Like she says, she'll come in handy for killing game. We can travel lighter when it comes to supplies."

She had a faint, funny smile on her pretty lips, like he wasn't telling the whole truth but she wasn't going to contradict him.

Well, all this left me so surprised I had my head full thinking about it. But I knew one thing. I was sure going along after Ike Tolbert.

Her being along clinched that.

CHAPTER 4

THE next day, though, something happened that changed Frank Ladd's plan. Buck Ardmore, marshal of Staffold, quit his job. And the town council was left with the problem of filling the vacancy.

Actually, Buck's badge didn't say he was the marshal—leastwise the one he'd had designed for himself didn't say so.

Buck was maybe thirty years old, and in keeping with his modern line of thinking he'd had a big gold-plated badge made up for himself that read Chief of Police, Staffold. At seeing it the first time you might have felt like laughing, since he was not only the chief, he was the entire police force.

But then, when you looked into his face, and particularly into his eyes, there was something that knocked the laugh right out of you. There was something in those eyes, so pale gray that from a distance of a few feet they looked like they were all white, that did that to you.

I'm speaking of this as if I knew it at the time I heard he'd quit, but that wasn't so, because I hadn't even seen him until after Frank brought the news of his resignation from town.

Lola and I were at the shack, planning what we'd need to take on the trail, me having slept behind the place the previous night and eaten a couple of meals she'd cooked.

"The marshal job is open," Frank said to Lola right off.

"Maybe you'd better apply for it, Frank," she said.

"Pays a hundred a month, which is some better than I've been making as a show horse," he said. "Ain't much to it, either, outside of running in drunks and busting up brawls."

"When's the last time you broke up a brawl, Frank?" she said.

"Why Lola, you know as well as me when that was."

"A long time, Frank, is what I'm thinking." She paused. "What I'm wondering is why Buck is giving the job up."

He looked down at his feet before he raised his eyes to meet hers again. "To tell the truth, he's going after Tolbert."

"And the big money," she said.

"Yeah," Frank said. "I guess I kind of forgot there'd be somebody else interested in that bounty. After all these years I got to thinking Tolbert would be mine to get."

I was real disappointed at the way he sounded. It was as if he'd lost the enthusiasm he'd had the day before.

"Marshal's job would mean security, Lola," he said. "And men like Ardmore taking off after Ike kind of cuts down the odds of me being the lucky one."

I thought she might argue, since it seemed to me that she was pretty impressed by that big bounty money.

But she said, "I told you to go ahead and apply for it."

He nodded, as if he was somewhat relieved. "You know, I think I'll do that," he said. "We could get along fairly well on what the job would pay, and I'd feel I was doing a man's job again."

Right then he went down several notches in my esteem. It just didn't seem right he'd settle for a job like that, not when we'd already made plans for the other. I could see then that the recent years of living without self-respect, finally working as "a glorified saloon swamper," had destroyed his pride.

And pride was what had made him a legend. With his pride gone, he would be nothing. I couldn't stand it. I said, "Frank, don't do it. I'll give you all the help I can, if you'll go for Tolbert. Even if we don't get him, the try will be worth it."

He looked at me for a while without speaking, then he said, "Yesterday I thought so. But with the marshal job up for grabs, I ain't at all sure."

I turned on Lola then. "Why do you keep telling him to apply for that tin badge?" I was mad as hell.

"Drew," she said, "don't be sticking your two-bit's worth into family business." Her tone was calm, without anger. In fact she was smiling faintly.

I couldn't see anything to smile about.

Frank looked from one to the other of us. "Might be well, Drew, if you was to go into town with me for a while. I don't want you two fighting over me."

"Do that, Drew," Lola said.

Well, if she wanted to get rid of me, so be it, I thought.

"McElroy owns the mercantile, heads up the town council," Frank said as we rode in, side by side.

We could have easy walked, but we were both horsemen and we'd rather saddle up than do so.

We stopped in front of the Staffold Emporium, which was McElroy's place. "Might as well come in with me," Frank said. "This may be the best thing that's happened to me in a long time."

It bothered me that he'd asked me along. A man of his stature I'd have expected to keep a discussion like this private. In the back of my mind, though, was a suspicion that maybe he didn't want me around Lola when he wasn't there. But maybe that was just my own vanity talking.

Anyhow, I went in with him, and the place was empty of customers. A gaunt, middle-aged man was behind one of the counters, wearing black sleeve protectors and a white apron. He watched us coming in without any expression on his face.

"Morning, Mac," Frank said.

"Morning, Frank."

Frank introduced me briefly and I shook hands. Then McElroy said, "What can I do for you, Frank?"

"It's about Buck Ardmore quitting."

"I guessed that."

Frank looked a little surprised, but he said, "I could hold down that job right well, Mac."

The merchant didn't say anything for a long minute. Then

he said, "You want to apply, Frank, there'd need be a council meeting, of course."

"Sure," Frank said. "Sure, I understand. Kind of a formality, I suppose."

McElroy looked uncomfortable. "Yeah, you might call it that."

"Wouldn't guess there'd be too much trouble there," Frank said. "They all know what I done in the past."

"Well, now, I don't know, Frank. You know how times have changed. That's why the council hired young Buck. He done considerable studying on how to enforce the law."

"Hell," Frank said, "what's to study about keeping law in a town like this? I had a half dozen jobs like it in my day."

"Sure, Frank. In your day."

"What's that mean? You think I couldn't handle it?"

"I'm not saying that. I'm just saying it's up to the council to decide."

"You've known me for near a year now," Ladd said.

"Sure, Frank. But you got to remember that all the time you've been in Staffold, you've been only a greeter at Morency's place."

I couldn't keep my mouth shut. "My God! what about his reputation?"

McElroy looked at me as if I should be seen but not heard, and he appeared thoughtful. "We'll take that into consideration," he said finally. "We'll call a meeting tonight."

Ladd seemed pleased. "Thanks, Mac. I hope you'll put in a good word for me."

Well, Frank may have been satisfied with that, but I wasn't so sure.

We both expected they'd notify him to attend their meeting, as soon as they settled on the time.

But they didn't.

Like I said, they didn't have the guts to notify him like

they should. He had to go around to that storekeeper, McElroy, and ask.

He asked me to go along with him when he went, and I knew then that he was worried about what the answer would be. The real tip-off was when he asked me to wait outside while he went in to talk to McElroy.

I waited impatiently on the porch of the mercantile, and it seemed like getting an answer was taking a hell of a long time.

When he came out, he looked as if he'd been physically wounded. Sick and in pain, almost like he'd taken a bullet in his gut.

He walked past me without saying a word and made two tries at getting up into his saddle, that's how bad he was feeling.

But he didn't say anything as we rode along home.

Not until I couldn't stand it any longer and said, "Well?"

"They turned me down," he said.

"I'm sorry," I said, but I wasn't really.

"I hate to have to tell Lola that," he said. "I hate that worst of all."

I had the feeling Lola wouldn't care, but I didn't say so.

"You'd be surprised," he said, "on how bad a man wants to impress his woman as he gets older. Has something to do with him losing face as soon as they get to know each other. It all starts out with him being her hero. Then, too damned quick, she finds out both his feet are made of clay, *caliche* mud to be exact.

"From there on her esteem is all downhill. In the end she feels at best only a irritated toleration for him, I reckon. At worst she holds him in contempt." He paused. "And in the end he don't rightly know how it all come about. It sure as hell wasn't how he wanted it."

CHAPTER 5

SO now it was decided for sure. We were going after Tolbert.
The question in my own mind was, Where?

Ever since they discovered Judge Farrell murdered in
Tucson and the authorities there had concluded it was Ike
that done it, he hadn't been seen by anybody. It was like he
had dropped off the face of the earth.

"Where do you think he went?" I asked Frank.

"I been thinking on it," he said. His face took on a
remembering look. "First place I thought of was the Pinacate
region, across the border. Part of the Great Sonoran Desert.
That's where I caught him before."

"You figure he'd run for there this time?"

"He might have. A man wants to lose himself real quick
after killing a judge in Tucson, the Sierra Pinacate is the
place to do it." He paused. "He can also lose his life real
quick there. It's rugged country, a nightmare of old craters,
barren rocks, and sand, and mighty damned few *tinajas* that
ain't empty of water most of the year. It's mostly in Mexico.
Not that that makes any difference, because it's uninhab-
ited."

"How come Tolbert ran for there in the old days?"

"Closest spot he could think of, I reckon. He'd been
robbing the Southern Pacific Rail Line out of Yuma. Got to
be a habit with him, damned near, and me and some others
were laying for him.

"We almost caught him doing a job, but he slipped away. I
got the jump on the others and trailed him in there."

"And got him," I said. It made me feel good to be able to
say that.

26

"I got him, but that damned Pinacate almost got the both of us." He paused again, then said, "Would have, too, if it hadn't been for Ike."

I gave him a questioning look. "For Ike?"

"He knew something about that country, although I never knew why or how. But I had him in shackles and we were on the long way out. Our canteens were empty and we and our horses were dying of thirst. That's when Ike talked me into a detour, saying he knew where there was a big *tinaja* might still have some water in the bottom of it, although there hadn't been any rain for God knows how long.

"Well, I agreed and he found it, and it saved my life as well as his." Still again he paused. "That's bothered me all these years, boy. Thinking how it was him that saved my life, even if it wasn't necessarily his willing."

"I can see how that might weigh on a man, all right."

"More than you know, boy, more than you know. Especially after that judge gave him that long sentence."

I said, "I guess he'd head there again."

"Would you? Why?"

"Something I read recent in a newspaper. About some people that made a study of criminals. They come to a conclusion that bandits fall into a pattern of operations."

"They did, huh? That some of this modern thinking I been hearing about?"

"I guess it is," I said. "What they think nowadays is that a criminal gets a habit of doing things a certain way."

"Think of that," Frank said.

"Seems like you kind of agree with the theory, since you were figuring he might head for the Pinacate again."

"I changed my mind, boy. I been thinking back over the years to the time of Tolbert's trial. And remembering something that came out during it. That Ike Tolbert is a half-breed. His mother was a Navajo Indian."

"A half-breed?"

"Yeah. Lucky he wasn't a full-blood. He'd never have lived through twenty years of being locked up."

"So?"

"My hunch is he didn't go south this time. I'm guessing he headed north for the Navajo country. Those Indians got eighteen million acres of reservation up there."

"A lot of country to hide in," I said.

"And a thousand canyons," Frank said. "It won't be easy."

I guess I didn't realize just how bad off the Ladds were until we started to get ourselves outfitted for the trail. They were flat-butt busted.

I had forty bucks I'd won in a poker game in Prescott before I got taken with the idea of going to shake Frank Ladd's hand in Staffold. And that wasn't going to help much.

What we needed was a horse for Lola, a pack animal, ammunition and grub, and some cash for possibles that might arise.

"Can you sell the house here?" I asked. I was careful not to call it a shack.

"Hell, Drew," Frank said, "we just been renting."

"You think that storekeeper, McElroy, might grubstake you?"

"Ain't likely," Frank said. "He don't figure I can handle a town marshal's job, he won't figure I got a chance to get Tolbert."

"What about Morency?"

"He's sore at me for quitting the greeter job."

"Listen, Frank," I said, "maybe if you offer him a cut of the bounty, he'd be interested."

He looked thoughtful, and Lola did too. They exchanged glances, then looked back at me.

"There's another thing too," I said. "If you get Tolbert a second time, you'll be bigger than ever, Frank. Morency could really have a drawing card if you went back to him."

"Hell, with that kind of money, I'd not go back. That's the whole idea, boy."

"You don't have to tell him that."

"Drew's right," Lola said.

"Besides," I said, "Morency's a gambler by profession. Taking chances is part of his business."

"I don't know," Frank said.

"He'd likely hedge his gamble with side bets on Buck Ardmore or others, so if you failed he'd come out even anyhow."

"I don't know why he'd go to all that trouble," Frank said.

I began to get mad at him. "You want to know why? I'll tell you. Because you're Frank Ladd, that's why!"

"You got a lot of confidence in me, Drew." He smiled faintly. "And that surely does make me feel good. Only I doubt Morency shares your feeling."

"Do like Drew is telling you," Lola said. "You go ask him, Frank."

"All right," Frank said. "I will. But don't be too disappointed if he turns me down."

You know, I was beginning to understand what he'd said about Lola and her finding out he had feet of clay. It was a shock to me, and I could understand what a hell of a shock it might have been to her. What I was feeling mostly was exasperation. It wasn't disappointment, because I hadn't reached the stage where he wasn't still a hero to me. I was just mad as hell because he seemed to have lost his pride.

"Go ahead, Frank," Lola said. "If we're going after Tolbert, we want to beat the others there."

"They don't know where he is," Frank said.

"Neither do you. But maybe you guessed right. If so, some others might have too."

"All right," he said. "Drew, you going with me to Morency's?"

There it was again, and in a way I didn't like it. It seemed like he was using me as a crutch or something. On the other hand, I wanted to go because I wanted to witness Morency's reaction when he asked him.

"I'm ready," I said.

Lola didn't say anything when we left. She turned away and began straightening up some little things around the room that didn't suit her. Busy work, I thought. She'll be killing time until we get back with the answer. Because she's pinning all her hopes on this one venture. It may be Frank's last chance, and hers too, to live a better life.

And I was all for that.

Morency's place was uncrowded. Not at all like the day I rode in and Frank was there as greeter. Of course, it wasn't Saturday, and that could make a difference. But I preferred to think it was because he wasn't there in his circus rig and duds.

Morency was standing at the back end of the bar, smoking a cigar and looking on. He had a hired bartender serving the few customers.

When he saw us come in, the cigar he had between his teeth began to agitate and his mouth worked. He reminded me of a dog working on a bone.

He was scowling.

I threw a side-glance at Frank, and I was proud of him. The minute we stepped through the doors, he stood straight and tall, his shoulders back, his gunhand brushing the walnut grip of his old Peacemaker, and his eyes were bold and arrogant.

I was proud of him, even though I knew he was acting a part. He looked at that moment like Frank Ladd ought to look. The way he must have looked in the old days.

His appearance had its effect on Morency too. I could tell, because the scowl left Morency's face, and all at once he was staring respectfully at Frank, and he raised a well-kept hand to remove the cigar from his mouth. He said, "Hello, Frank." He didn't bother to look at me.

"Ad," Frank said, looking at him eye to eye, "I've come to you with a proposition."

Morency said, "Well, I'm sometimes interested in propositions, Frank."

"In your office, Ad." Frank wasn't asking, he was telling.

"Sure, Frank." Morency turned and led the way to the back, and to a door marked Private. He opened it and went in and sat down behind his desk.

I hung back by the door, but Frank strode right over and stood straight as an arrow and said, "I'm going after Tolbert, Ad."

"I figured," Morency said.

If Frank was surprised, he hid it. He said, "What I need, Ad, is a stake."

"What's in it for me, Frank?"

"I need three hundred dollars."

The saloonkeeper-gambler nodded. "Like I said, what's in it for me?"

"You'll double your money if I get the bounty."

"*If,*" Morency said. "Well, Frank, that's too big a gamble."

"Goddammit! Ad, I got to go after Tolbert. Don't you see how that'd be?"

"Why?"

"I *got* to, that's all."

Morency surprised me then. He nodded again. "Yeah, I can see how that'd be, Frank." He paused. "But you're a hell of a poor risk, my way of thinking."

"You're not thinking right, then," I said.

He switched his eyes to me and gave me a long, appraising look. "You going with him?"

"I am. And Lola too." I don't know why I told him that.

"Lola?" He turned back to Frank.

Ladd nodded.

"I heard she was a shooter in a traveling show before you married her. Is that right, Frank?"

"What's that got to do with it?"

"I'm asking you a question."

"Yeah, she was. Little Sure Shot, they billed her as. Little Sure Shot Lola."

"And this young fella with you. What would you bill him as?"

"Just a helper," I said.

"You ever shoot that gun you're wearing?"

"I've killed my share of tin cans with it," I said. "That's all."

"At least you're honest about it," Morency said. "And you look rawhide tough." He turned back to Ladd. "This thing about Lola going with you, that's a thing I never heard of! It intrigues the hell out of me, Frank."

"You going to grubstake me, then?"

"I might. But it'll have to be at better odds. I'll lend you the money, not stake you. Which means if you fail, you owe me the three hundred, and you'll have to work it out here. If you get the bounty, I want the money back triple. Nine hundred bucks, Frank, take it or leave it."

Frank didn't hesitate a second. "Done!" he said, and held out his hand.

Morency gave it an indifferent shake. He went over to a safe in the corner and turned the dial and came back with the currency and handed it to Frank. "I don't think I'd be doing this, if it wasn't that bit about Lola's shooting. Like I said, that intrigues the hell out of me, Frank. I always did admire that girl."

Frank had been looking pleased, but when Morency said that, he scowled. "I've seen the way you've looked at her."

"You can't blame a man for looking," Ad said, and I felt an agreement there.

"Sometimes I do," Frank said coldly.

Cold enough to give *me* a chill, although it didn't seem to bother Morency.

Well, the money was enough to get us outfitted with what we needed, and Frank had some left over.

We had some riding to do to get to the Navajo country, since Staffold was down in the southeast part of the state. So a couple of days later we were on our way.

I got to thinking about the agreement with Morency. If Frank got the five thousand bounty, he'd have to give Morency nine hundred. If it took a month, he'd have to give me a hundred. So that left four thousand for him and Lola. But I guess that was a lot more than they had been close to for many years.

If he didn't get Tolbert, he'd be back working out the loan in the saloon, mostly for free, and they'd be destitute for sure. It was a big gamble for Frank, and I was determined to give him all the help I could. Him and Lola.

She had been telling the truth when she'd said she was trailwise. She was an old hand at riding, I could tell that, but I could also tell it had been a while since she'd done any.

The first couple of days whenever she dismounted, she walked like her new Levi's fit her too snug. And they did. But she never complained. And she did the cooking, which was what you'd expect a woman to do.

On the fourth day, somewhere up on the old Coronado trail, she did something you'd not expect her to do. She walked out into the piñons a little way while Frank and I were making camp, and she shot an antelope.

She wouldn't say what kind of shot she had at it, so I didn't know how good she really was with that 30-30 Winchester she had. But, sinking my teeth into that fresh meat, I had high compliments for her ability.

Frank had seemed right proud when she called us out to haul the carcass in, but it was what he said that I was to recall later. He said, "Drew, it surely is hell to get old."

I knew he couldn't be referring to Lola. Or to the antelope either.

We made fair time, considering there was considerable

climbing, and the high altitude after we went through the
town of Morenci took some getting used to.

When we'd gone through the town I'd asked Frank, "You
reckon this place was named after Ad?"

"Ain't no connection," he said. "It's just a coincidence, like
between you and that mad dog, John Wesley Hardin." He
paused. "Besides, it's spelled with a 'i', not like Ad's with a
'y'."

"The day they name a town after Ad," Lola said, "that'll be
the day."

"Wasn't for him, Lola, we wouldn't be here," Frank said.

"And we'll pay plenty for that."

"Wasn't no other way."

"I'm not blaming you, Frank. You did what you had to do."

It wasn't until we had passed the Painted Cliffs and still
had some way to go to reach Fort Defiance, that we discovered we were being followed.

It was Lola who discovered it. By that time there was no
doubt in my mind that she had sharp eyesight.

"Frank," she said, "We've got somebody on our trail."

"How do you know?"

"I got a glimpse of him twice now. One solitary horseman."

"We ain't the only ones know and use this trail," Frank said.
But I could tell he was bothered by what she'd told him. "You
able to tell who it was?"

"No. But he must have seen me looking at him, because he
disappeared real quick."

Frank shrugged. "Might be he didn't do that on purpose."

"Might be," she said. "There's one way to find out. Lay
over a spell and see if he catches up."

"Makes sense," I said.

We took a couple of hours rest at midday, just to see what
would happen.

Nothing did.

"Whoever is back there doesn't want to catch up," Lola
said.

"Looks like," Frank said. "Well, we'd best be getting on."
If he was bothered, he didn't let it show.

It bothered me some, but I pushed it out of my mind.

I guess Lola didn't see the rider another time, because she didn't mention him again.

Fort Defiance was located at the mouth of a canyon, in the eastern part of the reservation, almost on the Arizona-New Mexico line.

It had been there over a half century, first as an army outpost to try to control the raiding Navajos. As late as 1860 it had survived the attack of a thousand Navajo warriors.

Which gives you some idea of what those old Navvies were like before Colonel Kit Carson and his troops busted them in '64. I guess the few years they were penned at Bosque Redondo tamed them.

In those early days though, they were fighting sons of bitches like their cousins the Apaches. Now the fort was mostly used as the reservation agency headquarters. There was a three-story masonry school building there now, where some Navajo kids were being educated when the school authorities could catch them.

Like most Arizona forts, it was in barren surroundings, but there was water and forage near, which was probably why it was sited there. There was some old barracks and corrals and administration buildings being used when needed.

My understanding was that the post-traders who dealt with the Navvies at scattered locations over the reservation got their licenses from here.

There was considerable bustle about the place, wagons of trade goods coming in from Gallup or somewhere. Wagons of wool from Navajo sheep going out. And there was a mixture of whites and Navvies working or loitering around.

The Navvy squaws all wore the same kind of clothes, those brightly colored velveteen blouses and satin skirts. The bucks dressed pretty much like us, range clothes and Stetson-type hats.

"This is the jumping off place, I reckon," Frank said. "This is where we start trying to track Ike down."

I kept looking around the landscape, which at this point was mostly canyon walls rising to what I guessed was an endless plateau, and wondering how we'd even begin.

I was still looking when I heard Lola gasp. I turned and saw her gripping Frank by the arm. "There's Buck Ardmore!" she said.

"Damned if it ain't," Frank said. "So that answers your question as to who was following us."

"You knew it all the time."

"Nope. But I guessed."

I had seen Buck around Staffold before we left, so I recognized him. He was now tying up his horse and pack animals at a hitch-rack down the street from a trader's place, there being no room closer because all the space was taken.

Just as Lola spoke, he looked up and met our glances.

Like I said before, Buck was maybe thirty, with rugged good looks, except for those scary gray eyes so pale they seemed to have no irises.

He raised a hand in salute, and without hesitation came walking toward us.

We watched him come, and when he got close Frank said, "I might have known it was you sneaking along behind us."

Buck didn't grin, like another man might have. He said, "Makes sense, doesn't it? I got a lot of respect for your judgment in some things, Frank."

He turned then and nodded to Lola.

She just gave him a cold stare.

"I knew you'd be glad to see me," he said to all of us, but keeping his eyes on her. He still wasn't smiling.

Neither was she.

CHAPTER 6

I COULD see that there was no love lost between Frank Ladd and Buck Ardmore. And none either between Lola and Buck, at least not on her part.

I waited for Frank to ask him what he was doing at Fort Defiance, but when he didn't, I thought what a damned fool question that would have been. We all knew why he was here.

Buck didn't make any bones about it either. Right off, he came up with a proposition. "Frank," he said, "we haven't been friends, but I've always had great respect for what you did when you were in your prime."

All that did, of course, was make Frank scowl, and it came to me that Buck wasn't much of a diplomat.

He plunged right on, though. "The way I see it, you and I could team up together and run down Tolbert twice as fast and with half the trouble."

Frank kept scowling. "Get to the point," he said.

"A fifty-fifty split on the reward money," Ardmore said. "You can't be more fair than that."

"The hell I can't." Frank jerked his head toward Lola and me. "I've already got two partners."

Ardmore didn't even look at us. "For what they're worth," he said. "I'd leave them here to wait, while you and me bring Tolbert in."

"You ever do any bounty hunting before, Buck?"

"What difference does that make?"

"It's some different from walking a town every few hours. It's a whole different business."

"I don't see it that way at all," Ardmore said. "But then,

you've always been bullheaded about your way of keeping the law."

"What we're facing up here ain't a matter of law-keeping," Frank said. "It's manhunting."

Buck seemed to have paid no attention to what Ladd said, because he went right on with his own words. "Being a lawman nowadays is a big change from in your day, Frank. I'd think you would have learned that. Nowadays, there are ways of figuring out a criminal's mind. We've got new methods, new tools to work with. You need somebody young with you that knows them."

"I don't see the connection here," Frank said. "Not out in this godforsaken Navajo country."

"I guess there isn't one, directly," Buck said. "I was just pointing out that you're not the greatest partner I could choose."

"Why do it, then?"

"Because you know Ike Tolbert. At least you did once. So we both have got something to offer."

I couldn't see that. Not out here in this wild country of the reservation. Which was just about what Frank had told him.

Meanwhile I went on listening with interest. I was worried that maybe Frank would agree to some kind of split with Ardmore. If he did, I thought, there wasn't much use of us going after Tolbert at all, since his and Lola's cut of the money would be so small, what with Morency's stake in it and my wages.

But Frank said, "No, Buck. I've got to do this on my own."

"I might take a lesser share," Ardmore said. "Say one-third."

"You'd like to get Tolbert bad, wouldn't you?" Frank said. "You'd get mention in newspapers all over the country, even if you had to share it. Make you a big reputation, wouldn't it?"

"Why not?" Buck said. "You did it once."

"I aim to do it again."

"Why not make it easy on yourself, Frank. You help me, and I'll help you."

There was no doubt in my mind that Buck wanted to team up. He wanted it bad.

"Sorry, Buck," Frank said. "And I won't wish you good luck."

Those whitish eyes of Ardmore's seemed to be drilling holes into Frank. "By God!" he said. "You're going to wish you'd taken me up on this."

I knew something about the vast Navajo reservation myself. I'd got hold of a book about it a couple of years back when I spent a season herding sheep for the Condor Cattle and Land Company up out of Prescott.

It was a lonely life and the only thing that kept me from going loco, I guess, was the few books my predecessor left in the snug covered sheep wagon I inherited for living quarters. I spent some long hours reading, and one of the books I read was called *The Navajos,* written by a Presbyterian missionary who'd spent some time among them in the mid-nineties. I must have read it through a couple of times during the time I was herding the woollies.

So I had some knowledge about these people that might be useful, but I had never been even close to the place before we reached Defiance.

Neither had Ladd. Or Lola. Or, it appeared, Buck Ardmore.

Some of the statistics stuck in my mind. And some of the history of the Navajos.

I think the thing that surprised me most was finding out that before Kit Carson and seven hundred volunteer soldiers and Ute scouts went after the Navajos in 1863 and '64, they had been notorious raiders, just like their cousins the Apaches. In fact, back a century or two, they were the same people. Their language was so similar they could pretty well understand each other.

The Navajos had raided the Utes and the Pueblos, the Spanish and the Mexicans, and after the United States took over the Southwest, the whites.

They might not have been as cruel as the Apaches, but they were their equals when it came to raiding for sheep—and women. They had raised so much hell with the settlers of New Mexico that Kit Carson was finally sent in.

Carson whipped them into submission by killing off their sheep and ruining their corn and other crops. They were starved into surrender.

Then they were then rounded up and marched to the desolate holding reserve at Bosque Redondo and guarded by volunteer troops stationed at Fort Sumner. The barren plain along the Pecos could not support their numbers. Many died. After four years, the government admitted failure, and after the Navajos agreed never to raid again they were allowed to return to their homeland. They had lived up to their agreement since 1868 and they had learned a bitter lesson: they did not want to fight the whites, the *belecanas*, again—ever.

There was one exception, though. That was a few who had escaped capture during Carson's attack by retreating deep into the northern canyons above the Utah border. These remained arrogant and wild, and not too much was known of them and their descendants at the time the book I read was written.

If, in 1915, these Navajos still remained warlike in their feelings, they were only a small minority. The vast majority of the Navajos worked hard at herding sheep and raising crops where and when they could.

This didn't mean they had any great love for their conquerors. They had simply learned they must get along with them if they were going to survive.

Their principal contact with whites was at the handful of government-licensed trading posts scattered over their domain, most of which was now set aside as a reservation.

It reached from a little north and east of Gallup, New Mexico, to the Grand Canyon, and from Utah's San Juan River south almost to Flagstaff—twenty-eight thousand square miles of plateau, a lot of it barren, some scantily pastoral. Deserts, canyons of sandstone, mesas, and mountains, all in varying hues and colors, but all of it harsh to those not native to it.

And into this forbidding country Ike Tolbert had disappeared. At least we thought so. Or Frank Ladd did. But he was only working on a guess.

We hung around Fort Defiance a couple of days, asking questions but trying not to give away our reason for asking. We didn't have much success either way. Word about Tolbert's crime had reached the post, and somebody mentioned that he was part Navajo, and there was a guess or two that matched Frank's. But there was no real evidence.

The Navvies might have known, some of them, but we didn't know how to approach them.

It was Lola who finally made a breakthrough.

There'd been a lean young Navajo hanging around who'd seemed to have his eye on her. I'd noticed his hungry look whenever she passed him by, and I didn't like it a bit. I don't know if Frank noticed too, but if he did he made no issue of it. Maybe he just didn't want to start any trouble, figuring we had enough problems at the moment trying to get started on our quest.

Anyhow, Lola noticed, that was sure. And being Lola, she right away figured to use the Navvy's interest to try for information that we needed.

He spoke English like he'd learned it in one of the reservation schools when he was a kid.

But it was her that had started up the conversation with a Navajo word she'd already picked up:

"Yah-ah-tay," which means hello.

He looked surprised. I don't guess he'd had many white women initiate a conversation with him. But he was willing.

"Yah-ah-tay," he said, and added partly in English, "Pretty *belecana."*

That didn't fluster Lola at all. She went right after what she wanted to know. "Did you ever hear of a man named Ike Tolbert?"

"Sure," he said. "I hear something. He out of prison now."

"Did you know he was part Navajo?"

"Sure. He have white father, but Navajo mother. That make him Navajo."

She appeared to think about that. Maybe she hadn't known that among the Navajos a bloodline is traced on the woman's side.

"He was many year in those prison. Too many," the Navvy said.

"He did some bad things," she said, talking down to him as if he couldn't understand grownup English.

"Bad things? You mean rob trains? He don't think that bad. You know about railroads? The government they give them much Navajo land on each side of tracks when they build the Santa Fe."

"I heard."

"Ike Tolbert, he was farm, raise sheep on railroad land because at place he pick the soil is good. Railroad send men with guns, run him off, run his sheep through corn, ruin everything. Ike he go to get even."

Lola said, "But he was arrested after he robbed the Southern Pacific, not the Santa Fe."

"Sure. Ike he don't got prejudice. One railroad or other, he rob them both."

"Is he on the reservation now?"

"Why you ask?"

"I just asked."

The Navajo showed his teeth. "You don't fool me, *belecana."* He looked at Frank and me. "You all got guns. You come to look for Ike Tolbert."

"Is he a friend of yours?"

He didn't answer her at first. Then he said, "How he be friend of mine? Most my life he been in prison. I only know what I hear my people say."

Frank cut in then. He said, "We might need a guide."

"How much you pay?"

"Twenty-five dollars a week."

That jarred me, because that was as much as he was paying me. Before I could object, the Navvy spoke.

"All right, *Hosteen,*" the Navvy said. *Hosteen* was like mister.

I said, "Listen, Frank. You can't trust a Navajo to side with a white against one of his own people. I read that somewhere."

Frank ignored me. He said to the Navvy, "What name do the whites call you?"

"When I come here to the school as young boy, they give me name of Samuel. Samuel Begay. Better you just call me Begay. I don't like name Samuel."

I gave him a close look. He was one of the tall, slim-type Navvys, of which we'd seen many around the fort. His long black hair was tied up in a *chongo* knot beind his neck, and he wore Levi's, boots, a denim jacket over a wool shirt, and a cowboy hat. His skin wasn't any darker than mine was from the sun, but his eyes and features were pure Indian.

I said, "What're you doing hanging around the fort?"

"I don't have wife," he said. "I don't have sheep. Sometimes I get job here."

"Do you know the back country of the reservation?" Frank said.

"Sure I know."

"Twenty-five, then," Frank said. "But only if you ain't lying about the back country."

"Hell, Hosteen, all Navajo land is back country."

"You know what I mean."

"Sure I know. I ain't been stupid. When we leave?"

"Tomorrow," Frank said.

"I need gun."

"We got the guns. You do the guiding. We'll do the shooting."

I had the feeling Begay wasn't too happy about that, but he didn't show it on his face. It was a while before he nodded, though.

When we started the next morning, I still didn't know what our plans were, although I guessed Frank did, or I figured he ought to. And he'd bought a map of sorts at the trader's.

We lined up behind our Navvy guide, swung into our saddles, and with me leading the pack mule we went a few miles south before Begay turned west. We kept looking back. We didn't see Buck Ardmore, but we knew he'd be trailing us again.

I guess we followed a trail about thirty-five miles, and come late afternoon we reached a cluster of buildings that made up the Hubbell Trading Post at Ganado.

I'd read that Lorenzo Hubbell was one of the first traders to set up a fixed post to deal with the Navajos. He had learned to speak the Navajo language well, and was considered a friend by most of them.

He was part Mexican, on his mother's side, and his Navajo customers all referred to Don Lorenzo as Old Mexican, probably for that reason.

He was a friend to us also, putting us up for the night on his grounds and providing us with meals. He didn't bother us with annoying questions either. But I got the idea he was curious about what we might be after. One thing was sure—having Lola along would throw off any suspicion that we might be on a manhunt.

None of us, except for Begay, had ever been in a Navajo trading post, and at first sight it appeared to me like a confused jumble of chaos. It was only after you watched a while and saw there was a definite order and pace to the operation that you were surprised at how well it all worked.

Trade goods were piled in corners and hanging from

hooks in the beamed ceiling and from nails driven into the walls—harness and riding tack, hardware and tools like axes and saws and shovels, ropes, and lanterns. There were shelves of cloth for making women's clothing, bolts of velveteen and satin and cotton.

There were denim outfits for men, boots and shoes, and cowboy hats.

Here and there were stacks of rugs woven by the squaws and traded. Stacks, too, of foodstuffs: flour, coffee, sugar, and canned goods. And tobacco for rolling cigarettes, as well as the chewing kind.

There was an adjacent storehouse with stuff the Navvies had traded in, like sheepskins and piñon nuts. Some furs too.

There was also a separate room which was kept locked, and it contained the turquoise and silver jewelry that the Navvies pawned when they were hard up, but which they almost always got out of hock before the three-year period the trader allowed was up. If they didn't, he could sell it. Most of it was beautiful stuff, made by Navvy silversmiths, and I think Hubbell was pretty lenient about the deadline.

As were most of the other traders, I was told. There was a friendship between the Navvies and the traders that didn't exist with any other whites.

Hubbell told us that the post licensees were invariably white. The few times a Navajo tried to run a post he soon went broke because he had so many relatives who expected favors in the way of free merchandise.

The whites, of course, could steer clear of this problem. They kept accurate credit records, often on paper sacks stuck on a spike, and the Navvies, it appeared, made it a point to keep in good standing. They had great need of the services provided them by the traders.

We got a late start the next day, because Begay wanted to wait for the local Navajos to gather for trading. He said he'd try to find out what they knew, if anything, about Ike Tolbert.

So we waited a while, and sure enough they began to come in, and for me things really got confusing then. Believe me, a trader led a busy life, although in a measured pace.

When Begay called them locals, he had to be covering a lot of territory, because there must have been a couple of dozen crowded into the post. And when you looked out on the reservation you could look for miles and miles and never see a *hogan*. Some of them must have been riding since before dawn to get there.

Nobody hurried. Sometimes a Navvy woman would spend an hour choosing the color of a piece of cloth she wanted.

The men were just as choosy, or maybe just killing time. A post like this, I guess, was a social center for them as well as a supply house.

Begay mingled with them for more than two hours. Then, abruptly, he signaled to us he was ready to leave.

It wasn't until we were on the trail that Frank got him to open up and tell what he'd learned, if anything.

"He on the reservation someplace," Begay said. "I learn that."

"That's all?" I said.

"You got to understand a thing. Those people this morning, they don't been to school at all, mostly. They still scared of *chindi*."

"*Chindi?*" Frank said. "What the hell is that?"

"A *chindi* is a ghost of a dead people."

"What do you mean?" I said. "Tolbert isn't dead, is he?"

"Not *chindi* of him. They scared of *chindi* of man he kill."

"Of the judge?"

Begay nodded. "That the *chindi* they afraid of. His ghost maybe follow Tolbert. These no-school people, they scared. It worse because they hear he cut off man's head after he dead, they say. Nobody want to get close to Tolbert now. That ghost will come try to get his head back."

"Maybe they'll tell us where to find him," I said.

Begay shook his head. "You don't understand. They don't

help. Not white man, not *belecana* against Navajo. They know Ike been locked up for twenty year. That kill most Navajo. So they been sympathize with him. They maybe try protect him, but not up close. They don't want be there when that *chindi* of the judge come looking for his head and find them helping him."

"Where do they think he is?"

"They say they don't know. They say somebody seen him north of Many Houses. He got pinto horse he maybe steal. He got food and things. He got rifle too. He must been busy after he kill that judge." He paused. "Many Houses, that mean Flagstaff."

I said, "Anybody tell the Navajo police that he was seen?"

"You don't need worry about them. They scared of *chindi* like everybody else."

"How come you aren't?" I said.

"Hell, I'm educated Indian. I gone to school through six grade." He paused. "But I tell you, I don't come close to Tolbert, even so."

"*Chindi?*" I said mockingly.

"You *belecanas* think you know everything," he said.

Frank said, "Not all of us. How much do you know about Ike's background?"

"Background?"

"About him when he was young. Before he went to prison."

"I know he got a *belecana* father. I know he try farm, and railroad run him off. I know he rob trains. That's all."

"I'd like to know something about him," I said, "seeing as I'm helping to run him down."

"What Begay here says, is it," Frank said. "Except I know some of the details of it that came out during his trial. Things the newspapers dug up, mostly. What they call human interest stuff, I think."

He began to talk.

Begay listened, as intent on his words as I was.

Tolbert had been twenty-seven when he'd bungled the holdup of the Southern Pacific. And he'd been only two years gone from the plot of ground he and the rest of the Navajos considered part of their land.

His two-year spree of crime had been exaggerated by the newspapers of the day, especially those in the East, until those in the West couldn't ignore it.

Like Ladd said, there was human interest in the story. The simple young Navajo farmer and shepherd, tilling a piece of ground to plant corn, became in a matter of months the half-breed desperado wreaking vengeance on the powerful railroads.

It was Ike's misfortune that the spot he picked to farm belonged to the Santa Fe Railroad, which, as was the custom, had been allocated by the government a wide band of land on either side of its right-of-way.

And it was his further misfortune that the railroad's agents, Indian-hating hired bullies really, took it upon themselves to run him off his land and destroy his crop.

They had shown up one day, caught him outside his crude *hogan,* and told him to get off.

Ike, as a Navajo, saw the futility of arguing, but he argued nevertheless. After all, he was white on the side of his father, a second-rate painter from New York who had sojourned briefly in the Navajo country while trying with mediocre success to capture its vivid landscapes on canvas.

Joshua Tolbert's artistic enthusiasm was intense but short, as was his ardor toward the Navajo girl he took up with. He soon returned east with the intention of selling his works. He left behind him a grieving squaw, handsome of face and several months large of belly.

He never came back.

And now his son, with a latent dislike of whites aroused by abusive treatment, was beaten by the hired bullies and left huddled on the ground while his attackers ruined his holdings. They then told him not to return if he wanted to live. And they told him that was the order of the railroad.

It was a warning both railroads were soon to regret, as the half-breed son became more adept as a holdup bandit than his father had ever been as an artist.

When Frank finished, Begay nodded and said, "You see why the Dinéh, the Navajo people, they go to hide him if they can."

"In spite of the *chindi?*" I said.

He nodded again. "But they try not get close."

"And you? Why should we trust you to find him?" I said.

"Maybe I got reason my own."

"And what would that be?"

He didn't answer that. His face just took on that carved-wood look an Indian can get sometimes, and I knew it would do no good to repeat the question.

CHAPTER 7

AT Flagstaff, Ike Tolbert had stolen a saddled horse. It was a strong pinto gelding, chosen in haste from several hitched in front of a saloon at the north edge of the town.

It was a well-gaited animal, and it was only later that Tolbert had some regret over his choice when it came to his mind that a pinto stood out in appearance. That could be a disadvantage to a rider on the run.

By then, though, he was well on his way to the edge of the reservation.

For many days he had picked his way northward from Tucson, stealing horses to ride, then abandoning them as he neared settlements where they might be recognized. He had repeated this procedure several times, his idea being to forestall prolonged pursuit by the victimized horse owners. It was a bothersome way to go, but one he felt necessary.

His main fear was of being identified. In one small town he had seen a poster that carried his picture, taken years before at the time of his trial.

Luckily, the years and his confinement had changed his appearance enough that he went unrecognized by the town's marshal, into whom he'd blundered.

Now, leaving behind Flagstaff, which was called by his people Many Houses, he rode hard for the reservation boundary somewhere up ahead.

His people? It had been so many years since he had left them, and even then he was not really one of them. Not in his own mind. He was cursed with the blood of his *belecana* father, whom he had never known. Still, as a child, he'd been accepted by the People, for his mother's sake. Accepted by the Dinéh, as they called themselves.

The Dinéh, the People. The word came strangely to his lips. Once he had spoken his mother's language fluently, but now he had to dig for the words.

Still, they *are* my people, he told himself fiercely. On them he had to depend for help. They will not give me away to the white men, he thought. Never. No matter what.

But he *was* tainted by his white blood. Else he would have fled from the body of the judge as soon as he'd killed him. Fled from the *chindi*, the dead man's ghost. Only a white would linger to saw off his head with a knife and carry it in his hands to place on a gatepost. He was a white man when he did that. He'd given no thought to the act, driven as he was only by the desire for revenge for an unjust sentence.

Now he was bothered by what he'd done. It was a feeling that increased as he neared the land of his people.

It was as if by reaching there he would once again become as they were, vulnerable to all their old superstitious fears. Fears he had shed long ago, first and partially in those early years at the white man's school, and later and wholly at the white man's prison.

His changing feeling caused him to throw a nervous glance over his shoulder, and he saw there to his left the Navajo sacred mountain of the West, Dokoslid, more than two miles high, green-sloped and bald-peaked.

He kicked the pinto into a brief run. For a moment, before he got a grip on himself, he was wholly Navajo, trying to flee the *chindi* of the judge.

Once he checked his fear, he reined the pinto in. He had a long way to go. He'd not let foolish superstition destroy the horse.

He rode then at a mile-eating pace of alternate walk and trot, and his mind slipped deep into the past, where his troubles had their beginning.

Back to when he'd escaped the white man's school, where

he'd been held against his will, and fled to the fierce canyons of the north where his mother's people had lived in isolation since the days when they'd eluded Kit Carson's roundup.

Then, at twenty, no longer a target for zealous missionaries seeking children to convert and teach the white man's way, he had tired of the isolation and come out of the wild country to first work for, then inadvertently settle on the lands of, the whites.

He had planted his crops, acquired a few sheep, and had hoped to live in future prosperity by Navajo standards.

And then the hirelings from the railroad came, or men who said they were from the railroad. . . .

In those days it had been a generation since the Navajos had last been warriors. But Ike Tolbert became one, making war on the railroads.

To be truthful, he had enjoyed it.

But then had come the botched holdup, and his relentless pursuit by that bounty hunter into the desolate Pinacate, of which Ike had some knowledge from prior refuge there. And there had come his capture.

He'd heard the bounty hunter had become famous for what he'd done. What was his name? Ladd, Frank Ladd, that was it.

He wondered now what had become of Ladd. It had been years since he'd heard any mention of him at Yuma.

He'd not hated Ladd, had admired him even for his courage in tracking him into the Pinacate. Particularly since it was commonly believed that he, Tolbert, had threatened to never be taken alive, to kill without hesitation any man attempting to arrest him.

That was a newspaper fabrication. He'd never made such a threat.

Hell, when Ladd had cornered him, got the drop on him, he'd surrendered, expecting, naively, a short sentence, since he had good reason to prey on the railroads. Hadn't they ruined his farm?

Well, he'd learned better. Twenty years in those hellholes had taught him.

They'd never take him again. The fabricated threat of years before was real now, whether they knew it or not. He'd not go back to confinement, no matter what the cost. He'd kill any pursuer without qualms. Or die trying.

He came now to a weathered post with a sand-blasted crossarm that must have once been a sign. He guessed it marked the south boundary of the reservation.

He kicked the pinto forward, crossing that invisible line.

He savored then a feeling of sudden relief, as if he'd found a sanctuary. He knew this was foolish, but the feeling did not go away. Instead it kept growing with every mile he rode.

His people. But he began to worry then about how he would look to them. He had his mother's dark skin and her fine cheekbones. He was sparse-bearded and had an infrequent need to shave. When he looked into a mirror to do so, he saw the Indian cast to his features. But his eyes were a startling blue.

Thinking about this, he swore in the white man's language. "Goddam *belecana!*" he said. And then wondered if he was really cursing his father, or himself.

No. He was cursing the man who deserted his mother. He, Ike, was Navajo. The People would know that.

He had eaten in Flagstaff, buying the meal with what he had left of the money he'd taken from the house of the judge he'd killed.

Now he was hungry again, and thirsty too. There had been no water since he'd left the timber north of Many Houses.

He began searching either side of the trail for sign of some Navajo's hogan. At a distance, off to his right, he saw one with hexagonal circumference and rounded dome made of posts and poles and branches of foliage covered by dried mud.

He turned the pinto in that direction.

He'd see now if he would be accepted.

CHAPTER 8

"HE gone to back country, all right," Begay said. "Up north."

"Somebody tell you that?" Frank said.

"Somebody say maybe. I think that where he go, anyway. The people up there, they maybe don't hear what he done. So they don't be afraid of *chindi*."

"That makes sense," I said.

"Well, let's get going then," Frank said.

"We be some days to get there, Hosteen."

"So, let's go."

Ever since we'd left Fort Defiance, Lola hadn't been saying much. Ever since we'd reached the Navajo country she'd been strangely silent. It was if she was awed by the vastness of it. Then too, I could tell she didn't trust the Indian.

I didn't either. Frank, he just sort of accepted him as a necessary evil, someone we needed but would have to watch. Not that he put this into so many words. It was just that I could sense he wasn't about to be taken in by Begay if he could help it.

Another thing I didn't trust about the guide was the way he looked at Lola sometimes. It made me mad as hell because I knew exactly what he was thinking. We were about the same age, and I could read his mind. Hell, our thoughts had to be near identical.

If Frank noticed this he sure didn't show it. I guessed that when you reached the age he was maybe you just didn't pay that much attention to such things.

But I knew Lola could read Begay's mind too. I suppose any woman could have. She read mine also, but she usually had a smile for me. But I'd never seen her smile at the Navajo.

He'd better keep his damned hands off of her, was what I was thinking.

He was a good guide, though, I had to say that for him. At least he seemed to know the country. We'd have been lost for sure if it hadn't been for him.

When Frank had first said we'd go look for Ike on the Navajo reservation, I guess I'd been thinking of someplace small. That's until I remembered reading that it was bigger than the states of Vermont, Rhode Island, and Massachusetts combined.

Without Begay we wouldn't have know which way to start.

Although I had some doubt if Begay really knew either.

But at least he acted like he did. He took the trail west toward Tuba City, more than a hundred miles away. It was a wagon road.

We stopped at Keams Canyon, then went on past Indian villages with names like Shongopovi and Oraibi.

I noticed Begay didn't seem to want to waste much time near these places. He finally muttered that these were Hopi villages, and that the adjoining mesas were all part of a block of land the government had given the Hopis right in the middle of the Navajo reservation. There wasn't much love lost between these two tribes, and he hurried us on through.

The next day we reached Tuba City, which wasn't a city at all. I asked Begay how it got its name, and he said it had been founded many years ago by a Mormon who had been befriended by a Hopi headman named Tuba. It was a Mormon settlement for several years. There were several springs in the area, he said.

There were irrigation ditches on either side of the main dirt street that the Mormons had built. The ditches were lined now by tall poplars.

There was a trading post here too, and a boarding school for Navvy kids, and a building that quartered the Indian

Bureau agent for this western part of the reservation. The agent was gone off somewhere on agency business, and the day after we got there we left without seeing him.

Begay led us out on a trail that went east.

Frank scowled. "You got someplace in mind?" he asked Begay. "Or are you leading us back to where we came?"

"I got a place," the guide said. "We go north soon."

"Tell me about it."

"Tolbert maybe go for Navajo Mountain. It sacred place."

"He got kinfolks near there?"

"That where he born, I think."

"Does he speak Navvy?" I asked.

"I think he forget much, maybe, remember some."

Lola said, "All the years I've known about Tolbert, I never thought of him as an Indian."

"Once Navajo, always Navajo," Begay said. He didn't grin when he said it. In fact, he had a frown on his face, like it was something that bothered him. It made me wonder whose side he'd be on in a showdown, even though he'd hired on to track Tolbert down.

"Even if he's half white?" I said.

"Make no difference," Begay said. "Especially when he Dinéh by his mother."

"You must be a matriarchal society," Lola said.

Begay looked blank. "I don't know that. But Navajo woman have big say. She own family sheep. She get mad at husband, she put his saddle outside hogan door, he finished."

"Finished? You mean divorced?"

Begay considered the word, then said, "Yes. That it."

"You hear that, Frank?" Lola said.

Frank turned his head to stare at her. He said nothing.

"Woman keep children," Begay said. "Keep hogan. Keep sheep too. Man only keep horse and saddle she put out."

That did it. Frank said, "Lola, don't get any ideas."

"Why, Frank! Are you worried?"

He didn't answer her. She may have been teasing him, but he wasn't taking it lightly.

I couldn't blame him for that. Not when I was wondering myself what was going through her mind. It excited me.

"This country we go to," Begay said, "it have Navajo name of *Not-sis-ahn.* It mean Hiding Place from Enemies. Many canyons where Ike's people come to hide from Kit Carson. In middle is sacred mountain, same name. It protect them."

"How interesting!" Lola said.

Begay gave her a long look, then said, "It maybe protect Tolbert."

Frank said, "You people are kind of superstitious, ain't you?"

"Missionary tell me that one time at school," Begay said. "He say only fool believe what Navajo believe." He shrugged. "Navajo believe what he believe. Sometime he believe missionary too, but he don't forget what he believe before."

We rode in silence for a while, then Begay spoke again. "The Dinéh in those canyon, they never been beat by white soldiers. They still like Navajo warriors in the old days. We got to be careful with them."

"You trying to scare us?" Frank said.

I remembered what I'd read. "He's right, Frank. In the old days they attacked Utes, Pueblos, Mexicans, sometimes even Comanches."

"That seems hard to believe, nowadays."

"Just remember they're the same breed as the Apache," I said.

Begay was listening to us. He said, "Maybe you believe when we get there."

"Maybe I will," Frank said.

We crossed a long, sandy stretch that was slow going. It took us a day to reach a dry lake bed below the sloping side of a sandy mesa. To the east and north was the rim of a whitish mesa rising high above a broad stretch of sagebrush flat.

The next morning Begay took us past twin formations of sandstone that looked like a giant elephant's feet. We climbed to higher terrain and the trail led north over endless rock beds that made it treacherous going for the horses. It was isolated country if I ever saw any.

At the middle of the day after the next we got our first glimpse of the sacred mountain Begay had spoken of.

He signaled a halt and pointed at it with his chin, the way the Navajos have of doing. That's because they figure using their finger to point at anybody can also point them out to witches or bad spirits or something. I guess the habit carries over to even pointing at a mountain or such.

Anyway, he said, "Not-sis-ahn. Navajo Mountain."

Looking at it from the south the way we were, it didn't look all that impressive. Not from a distance.

It took us a lot of miles of riding to get close. It was more impressive then. It was surrounded by rugged canyons that seemed to spoke off of it, like it was the immense hub of a gigantic wagon wheel.

"It been a week, Hosteen," Begay said. "You pay me twenty-five dollar."

Frank looked startled. "You'll get paid when you've done the job."

"Done now," Begay said.

"Like hell. You hired on to help me find Tolbert."

"No, Hosteen. I hire to lead you where he is. You find him."

"I don't know this country."

"You got problem."

Frank got mad. "So have you. No money."

Begay's face looked like it was blasted out of tan sandstone. "Twenty-five dollar, Hosteen. Now."

"Give it to him, Frank," Lola said.

Frank dug into a pocket and came up with some sweat-soiled bills. I knew he couldn't have many left out of Morency's loan.

He counted out twenty-five dollars and thrust it toward Begay. Begay took it and shoved it into a pocket of his Levi's. He turned toward his horse.

Lola said, "Begay!"

He turned back to face her.

"We need you," she said.

"You got two men."

"I'm afraid out here without a guide."

"Too bad."

They were staring at each other now. Begay's expression changed under the look she was giving him. It was a look that shocked me. Then I thought, she's got to be acting. That tour she did in show business must have taught her how.

Or maybe just being a woman did it.

She said, "I need you, Samuel."

Interest flared in his dark eyes.

I almost had to laugh. Of course I knew back at Fort Defiance that she'd aroused his interest. What I witnessed now was how easy a beautiful woman can make a damned fool out of any man.

He fell for the trick, but he still wasn't stupid. "Twenty-five dollar not enough now," he said.

"We can make that thirty from here on," she said. She didn't take her eyes off of him. "We can, can't we, Frank?"

Frank grunted something that sounded like assent.

Begay kept looking at her too. "You say yes, Hosteen?"

The answer came as a snarl. "Yes, goddammit!"

"All right," Begay said. He was a long time breaking off his stare at Lola. He looked her up and down as if now he owned her.

I didn't feel like laughing then. And I was half mad that

Frank had given in so easy. Little by little my admiration for him seemed to be lessening.

Still, I was glad we'd have a guide. You could get lost and maybe die in that maze of canyons up ahead. Especially if you were on the trail of a native to the region like Tolbert.

Although how much of it could he remember after twenty years of confinement?

Another thought struck me that I didn't like at all. Maybe Lola wasn't acting when she flaunted that promise in her eyes at Begay.

That was something to think about.

CHAPTER 9

WE found out pretty quickly why Begay had wanted to leave us. We were being watched, and he knew it.

In all that chopped-up mix of ridges and colored chasms of red and tan and yellow and white sandstone, I hadn't seen a single hogan since before we'd sighted the mountain. I don't think Frank or Lola had either.

But Begay must have. Either that or he sixth-sensed they were there but hidden. Even so, you'd have expected to see smoke from cookfires in that clear air. But there was none.

He began getting edgy right after Lola conned him into staying.

We made camp that first night there at the mouth of a canyon where there was some sparse graze for the horses, although it was plenty scanty. There was old sheep sign that I recognized, and that was the reason. The place had been overgrazed, like a lot of the Navajo land we'd ridden over these last few days.

Here it was even poorer. Navajos living in these sparse reaches must have a hard life, I thought. And a hard life made for a hard people.

It made me think about what I'd heard of our own hill-folk back East in the southern Appalachians, and how after years of isolation they resented any intrusion by outsiders.

I had an idea it'd be no different with these Navajos who had been hiding here for the fifty years since fleeing from Kit Carson's volunteer ravagers. They'd likely have long-smoldering memories.

It was no wonder that Begay was growing spooky, guiding

a trio of armed whites who were out to get one of his Navajo kin.

His edginess was contagious.

Pretty soon it got to Frank, and he began to swear. "Dammit! Begay, you're as jumpy as a bit-up bull at fly time."

If Begay understood he made no comment. And while we were making camp, with Lola piecing together a meal while it was still light, he kept off by himself. His eyes kept studying the surroundings.

Then, after it got dark and the day's heat changed to the night's high altitude cold, he stayed clear of the small fire we'd built of greasewood branches.

Only once did he come close, and said something in a low voice to Lola. She shook her head, and he went away.

That worked on me until I couldn't stand it. I went over to her and asked what he'd said.

"He told me not to get near the fire. That I made a target."

"You didn't move," I said. I wasn't sure she was telling the truth.

"I'm taking the chance," she said. "To keep warm."

"That all he said to you?"

"What else?"

"I don't trust him."

The fire was burning down for lack of fuel, but there was enough light to reveal her smile. "Drew," she said, "I think you're jealous."

I didn't deny it. I noted that Begay had warned only her of the danger. He might be hoping Frank and I would die. That would leave him alone with her. I was damned sure he would like that.

And I took it as a personal warning of what we might expect from him.

Nothing happened that night. I guess Navajos are like most Indians in staying out of action during darkness. A lot of them have a fear of being killed fighting and wandering forever in a shadowland or something. But the fear was even worse with the Navvies, because they believed the land was full of *chindis* roaming around at night, and they damned sure didn't want to meet face to face with any. It seemed to me that the Navajos must be the most superstitious of all Indians. And for me that was hard to figure because of them being originally the same people as the Apaches. And the Apaches, to my knowledge, didn't believe in much of anything, although they did have a god they called Yosen, or some of them did.

Of course, when daylight came things could be different.

And they were.

The first difference was a rifle shot that kicked apart the little fire I'd rekindled to make coffee.

It kicked up some loose gravel that drove the twigs and branches flying, upset the pot, and sent us diving for the cover of a few rocks that surrounded us.

Lola and I ended up behind the same jutting chunk of limestone. I'd grabbed her up as I went for cover, dragging her with me. I landed sprawled with her in my arms, which was what I'd been wanting to do ever since I'd met her. But not under these conditions.

Surprisingly, there was just that one shot at first. Begay and Frank were a few yards off on either side of us, and the way the formations were, not visible.

I did something crazy then, considering the circumstances, I kissed her hard on the lips and hugged her to me. I mean, I *hugged* her. Maybe the danger stimulated me. Maybe it was just because I'd never got this close to her before.

She twisted her mouth free and said, "Drew! are you crazy?"

I paid no attention to her words.

She brought me to my senses then. We were lying on our sides, facing each other, and she brought her knee up hard into my groin, and I let go of her in a hurry.

Just then another bullet whined off the stone outcrop that

shielded us. She did something then that hurt me worse than her knee had done. She laughed at me.

She kept laughing as if she couldn't stop, hysterical maybe, but it cut me deep.

I was about to slap her, when she moved close again and planted her own quick kiss on my mouth. I grabbed at her, still hurting, but she rolled away.

"Drew," she said, "you're a caution."

At that moment a barrage cut loose that sent slugs ricocheting off the rocks around us.

"Poor shooting," Lola said.

"Scare shooting," I said. "A warning to back off."

"Do you think so?" She was taking me seriously now.

"They'd not waste cartridges on these rocks if it wasn't."

"Who is they?"

"Navvy kinfolk of Tolbert's," I said. "I've been expecting it."

"We'll not back off," she said. "I want that reward, Drew."

"Means a lot to you, doesn't it?"

"Believe me, it does. I'm tired of living poor."

"I read a book about how mercenary women are," I said. I was still mad about that knee in my genitals.

"You did a lot of reading in that sheep wagon, it appears."

"There weren't more than a dozen books. But I read them all twice."

The shooting had stopped again.

"What now?" she said.

"They'll be saving their ammunition for a better shot."

"You think they'd kill us to stop us?"

"I know it." I wasn't sure of this, of course. But it damn well could be true.

"What will we do, Drew?"

I shrugged. "Frank's in charge here."

"*He'll* think of something," she said.

The way she said it didn't make me feel any better. As if he was a man who'd find a way, and I wasn't. Which was true enough. What the hell, he was Frank Ladd wasn't he? And this was his business. Or at least it had been in the old days.

He wasn't long in making a decision. He called it out so we could hear. "We'll try another canyon."

I called back, "What difference will that make?"

"Somebody don't want us up this one. And we really don't know why."

"I got a good guess."

"Maybe they just don't want intruders," he said.

"Maybe they're hiding Ike."

Frank hollered over to Begay. "What do you think, Begay?"

Begay didn't answer at once. Then he yelled, "Maybe so, maybe no!"

I could hear Frank cussing in a loud voice. He said something that sounded like, "You want a straight answer, don't ask a goddam Indian!" Then he called to me, "Drew? Like I said, we'll try another one of these canyons."

I didn't have any ideas of my own, so I wasn't going to argue. Besides, I still had an awful lot of confidence in his ability. A man is your idol for twenty years, you don't shake it off just because you begin to see a crack or two in his image.

We spent some time peering out from our cover, trying to see if the shooters were still up the canyon, but we wouldn't see anything. We didn't hear anything either.

The waiting was getting on my nerves. Besides, Lola kept giving me an appraising look, like she was expecting me to do something. At least I thought so.

It was more than I could abide. I stood up, then caught her eyes with mine. "Somebody's got to find out," I said.

"You're a brave man, Drew," she said.

She said it just in time, because my nerve had just deserted me and I was about to drop back down behind our cover. My courage came back and I walked in the open over to where the horses were picketed. I picked up my saddle and threw it on my mount.

Nothing happened to me, and my confidence grew.

Frank came out then and joined me. "Must be what they want," he said. "Want us to leave."

"By God! I hope so," I said. I wiped a lot of sweat off my forehead with my sleeve.

We were all pretty leery as we got ready to go. Begay saddled Lola's horse before I could do it, then his own. He left me to get the pack on the mule. Now that he knew we needed him, he was quick to take advantage of it.

There was no more shooting, but we all expected there would be if we turned up the canyon again.

We didn't waste any time leaving. The first hundred yards I had that cringey feeling between my shoulder blades. As usual I was at the drag with the pack animal, Begay up front ahead of Frank. Lola was directly ahead of me, and I kept close behind her, wanting to shield her from any shots, even though the thought aggravated the sensation along my spine.

When the shots didn't come, I relaxed and began thinking about the way she'd kissed me on the mouth. Believe me, that was something I enjoyed thinking about. It held out a promise for the future that damned near set me on fire. Of course, at twenty-five, I didn't need much.

We came to the entrance of the next canyon that fingered off the escarpments of the mountain. Frank called something to Begay and Begay turned in and halted.

I pulled up past Lola and said to Frank, "This one?"

"Good as any, ain't it?"

"Could be bad as any too."

"Chance we take," he said.

It occurred to me then that if we got killed he wouldn't be losing near as many years as I would. Or Lola, either.

We had a hell of a lot more to lose than he did, I thought. But all I said was, "I guess you're right."

"We'll soon know," he said.

I'll admit I was scared going up that canyon. Hell, it looked just like the one we'd left. I wasn't only afraid for me. I was even more afraid for Lola.

My fear grew when Begay dropped back and left Frank out in the lead. I heard Frank start to argue, but Begay ignored him.

He rode beside Lola for a spell, but she didn't say anything to him, and after a while he stopped and let me catch up to him. I went right on by with the pack animal and he still sat there. Only after there were a few yards between us did he start forward again.

That made me mad, but I couldn't really blame him. His stake in this venture was even less than mine.

Of course there was his interest in Lola, but there was no way it could match mine, of that I was sure. I couldn't believe he could feel more than a fleeting lust for a white woman.

My own lust was different. I believed that.

As it turned out, Begay had put himself into the front line. Because when the shooting started it came from behind us.

For a second I almost laughed as I turned in my saddle and saw him glance back once, kick in his heels, and come racing toward us. He was one scared Indian, I thought. But a moment later I was one scared white man, as he overtook me and tore by.

I gigged my own horse, but the damn pack mule balked and there was a short tug-of-war before I could get going. I threw a glance over my shoulder and glimpsed some powder smoke near a brake of juniper, but I wasn't about to stop and try any saddle shots.

Up ahead the walls rose steeply on either side, but with some loose talus at the base just where the canyon crooked to the right. That's where we headed.

There was a scattering of rifle-fire that kicked up sand around us. It was poor shooting again, or maybe the same Navvies just trying to warn us.

I didn't have time to waste pondering which.

We reached the bend and rushed around it. The horses

were breathing hard. It had been tough going for them in the sandy bottom.

We found some protection among the talus rocks.

"Damn near outsmarted yourself," I said to Begay. "Changing from the lead."

"I know they following."

That stopped me. Maybe he did.

"I try tell Hosteen maybe we in box canyon. He don't listen."

"Are you sure?"

"Not sure. It have look like up ahead."

"If it is, we'll play hell getting out of this one."

He nodded. "You tell Hosteen."

I looked over at Frank, and knew by his scowl that he'd been listening.

He said, "He was a little too late in his warning. I was thinking about turning back. Then the rifles started cracking." He paused. "He could be right, though. Looking up at rimrock, we just might be caught in a blind alley."

"How do we get out?"

"Turn and fight, I reckon."

"By the sound of those guns, we're outnumbered."

He gave a short nod. "We'll make a stand here. Wait and see if they'll come in after us."

"They could wait us out forever."

"They're Indians," Frank said. "Indians don't have much patience when it comes to fighting. They want fast action and get it over with."

Well, I'd read that too. Indians were hit-and-run fighters. At least in the old days. After all, war was a game to them. That's why they'd been fighting each other for hundreds of years before the white men came. These Indians though, these modern-day 1915 Navajos, you could only wonder about.

But sure enough, they must have got impatient quick,

because we were no more than settled in when they rode into sight, with one of them holding up his hand in a peace sign.

"Don't shoot!" Begay said. "I talk to him."

"All right," Frank said.

Begay stood up and returned the peace sign. He was unarmed, but Frank and I had our weapons at the ready.

Frank said, "Go ahead, Begay."

Begay started walking out toward the Navvy leader who had stopped and was waiting. He went out without even asking for the loan of a handgun.

I guess he had no stomach for fighting his own people. Whether they had the stomach to shoot him remained to be seen.

I had another thought just then. Did Lola have what it took to kill? I glanced over at her. She was gripping her Winchester, but so far she hadn't drawn a bead on anything. I liked to think she was reluctant. I mean, she was a woman, wasn't she?

Part of my feeling, I think, was that I wasn't sure I was ready to kill a Navvy myself. Shooting old tomato cans was one thing. Taking a human life was another.

There were three mounted bucks waiting in sight as their leader rode forward to meet Begay. Each of them held a rifle crooked in his arm.

Begay and the Navvy leader had what seemed like a hell of a long discussion. Then Begay turned and trotted back toward us. I was surprised when the Navvy stayed where he was.

When Begay got within shouting distance, he called to Frank, "He say, what we want in their land here?"

"All that talk to say that?"

"I say you the law. You been send for find man kill judge."

"Good!" Frank called.

"He say he know that. But Tolbert one his cousins. He say you go away and forget, then there no trouble. Ike stay here rest of life. He don't go back to kill no more white judges. He been satisfy now."

"Tell him there are other lawmen will be after Ike. He's got to come in."

Begay shook his head, but he began calling in Navajo again. The leader answered, and Begay yelled to Frank, "He say he tell them the same. Go away and forget."

"Tell him the Navajo police will come."

Begay shook his head. "He know better. No Navajo police take Ike. They Dinéh. Cousins, maybe."

There was a silence, then the Navvy yelled again.

"Well dammit! What did he say?" Frank called.

"He say this blind canyon, like I think. No use go up."

"Why's he worried then?" I said.

Begay didn't answer me. Instead he went on, "He say we come out, he let us leave."

I said, "Frank, Ike must be up this canyon!"

"I think so, too," Frank said.

Begay said, "Hosteen, they going attack us, we don't leave."

"They'll lose some men if they do," Frank said.

"That don't stop them. They like old Dinéh. Warriors." Begay paused. "They kill you *belecanas*." He paused again. "And they take your woman."

I could tell that was going to bring Frank around. At least I was hoping it would.

"All right!" he yelled, and moved out of cover.

A rifle sounded from above us on the canyon rim, and the Navvy leader pitched out of his saddle.

The others looked up, wheeled their mounts to run.

They hadn't even got started before their horses were running with empty saddles. It was the best shooting I'd ever seen. And it all came from the rim up there.

I looked up, and I saw him. Buck Ardmore was standing in plain sight, looking at us. Then he raised his rifle, held it horizontal above his head in a kind of victory symbol. A second later he disappeared.

"You see him?" I said to Frank.

"I saw him," Frank said. "The sonofabitch helped us out of a tight one that time."

Begay was staring out at the fallen Navvies. He had a sick, terrified look on his face.

I could guess what he was feeling. These were some of his own people lying dead out there.

Besides *that* feeling, he really had some *chindis* to worry about now. After all, he was the one who'd led us into this country.

Frank and I both edged over close to Lola. Begay stayed as if frozen where he was.

"Why did he do it?" Lola said. "Why did he kill those Navajos?"

"He guessed maybe they were about to attack us," Frank said.

"But we were going to leave!" Lola said. "There was no need for that killing."

"He didn't know that."

"Why would he help us? Just because we're white?"

Frank shrugged. "I never liked Buck. He's got mean eyes, killer eyes, no matter how he talks about modern lawdogging. Still, he might have done it because we're white." He paused. "More likely, he's using us to track down Tolbert for him. Hell, he's never been more than a town marshal. You think he'd ever locate Ike in this kind of country?" He paused again. "No, the sonofabitch is using us for a bird dog."

"A bird dog?"

"He wants us to find Ike for him. When we do, he'll try to take him from us."

"How could he do that?" I said. "Three or four of us against one."

"Didn't you learn anything from the way he massacred those Navvies?" Frank said. "The sonofabitch is a killer. For five thousand dollars, he'd do the same to us."

That was enough to make my blood run cold.

There was another thing, more immediate. Ardmore had disappeared, and left us looking like the ones who had committed the slaughter.

And that could bring the whole Navajo nation down on us.

CHAPTER 10

BEFORE we left the bodies I rode over to look at the weapons they had. The leader had a Winchester 44-40 similar to my own. I took it off of him, along with a belt of spare cartridges he had. I took the cartridges and the carbine and rode back to where Begay sat his saddle, watching me.

"It's time you had a carbine," I said.

"No, no!" he said.

I pulled my own carbine from its scabbard. "I give you mine," I said. I held out to him. He looked at the one I'd taken from the Navvy corpse, and it was as if he was staring at a rattlesnake. Then he looked at mine. After a moment he reached out and took it. He nodded then. *That* one was all right with him. No *chindi* there, I thought.

"What now?" I said to Frank.

He said, "I don't think you ought to've give him that."

"I do," I said.

"You going to start bucking me, Drew?"

Well, I hadn't reached that stage yet. I said, "No, Frank, I'm not bucking you. It just seems to me he's earned the right."

"I ain't so sure," he said. "But we won't argue about it."

To tell the truth, I was already wondering if I'd made a mistake. But I wasn't going to admit it in front of Lola, who was watching the two of us with a curious interest.

I said again, "What do we do now?"

Frank said, "Those Navvies that Ardmore killed, they wanted awful bad to keep us out of this canyon. Could be that Ike's got a camp up there somewhere. We'll go find out."

There were some tracks here and there around us, and

there was also a lot of rocky bottom where a rider would leave no trail. We didn't spend much time looking, just headed up the canyon, with Frank now in the lead. I noticed Begay kept searching the ground with his eyes, but he didn't say anything. Again, I got the feeling I might have made a mistake in giving him my carbine. If so, it was too late to get it back without making myself a damn fool in Lola's eyes.

The canyon was blind, all right. We must have gone in six or eight miles before we came to an abrupt end. The walls were perpendicular all around us, at least two hundred feet high, and impossible to scale.

The canyon was also empty. So much for Frank's guessing, I thought. I said, "Well, Frank?"

He didn't answer me. He just kept staring at those walls on either side and at the end too. Like he was searching for a way out of his mistaken guess.

Lola and Begay were both silent.

Frank's eyes had stopped roving, and I looked to see what he found so interesting. And then I saw it too.

To our left, fifty feet above the canyon floor, at the end of a ledge that led from the corner made by the chasm's end, was a dark spot that appeared to be a fissure. It was deep enough that it might be the mouth of a cave.

Frank's glance went then to the box end of the ledge. There was a talus of fallen rock slanting up to intersect it.

Above the talus was an unclimbable wall.

"I want to see what that hole is," Frank said.

"What for?"

It might be a way out of this canyon."

"For who?"

"Tolbert."

"With a horse? Up that rock slide?"

"Might be done."

"Not without wings."

He rode close then to the foot of the talus, and I followed.

He studied the slide for a while, then said, "See those marks? Shod hooves made them. Surprising what a man can do if he has to. And a horse too, if he's made to."

"Why would he tug his horse up there?"

"Means one thing. He saw or heard us coming. And there's another end to that hole."

"A tunnel?"

"Most likely a natural cave, eroded by storm runoff over the centuries. You find them here and there in canyon country like this."

"He could have just climbed up there and shot at us."

"And leave his horse? He's on the run, Drew, and a man on the run is thinking of that first and foremost." He paused. "And he must have known damned well he'd not likely get a shot at all of us."

"He can be waiting in there now for us, horse and all," I said.

"He can."

"Well?" I had to wait for his answer.

"I'm going up there," he said finally.

"You'll be taking a chance."

He shrugged. "I want you and Lola to keep me covered. He'll have to show in that entrance before he can draw a bead on me. If he does, you've got him."

"And if he doesn't show?"

"I'm going in after him."

Lola had drawn close to us and was listening. She said, "Drew, he may need help up there. You've got to go with him."

Frank didn't say anything.

"You'll be alone with Begay," I said, hoping she'd get my meaning.

I guess she did, because she gave a light laugh. "I can take care of myself," she said. She reached down and patted her rifle scabbard.

Begay made no comment.

"All right," I said.

We picketed the horses. Frank and I took only our holstered handguns and began the climb up the talus.

It was tough going for Frank, although it didn't bother me too much. But a man would have to be damned desperate to try to coax a horse up there. Which, of course, Tolbert undoubtedly was.

When we got to a height even with the end of the ledge, we would see where he'd managed to lead the horse out on it. It was maybe thirty feet across to the fissure, and just barely wide enough for the animal to pass over, squeezed against the cliff face.

That is until they'd got out near the halfway mark. There we could see where the sandstone had given way under the horse's weight.

It had broken off for a couple of yards, leaving only a width of maybe six inches. I looked down and I could see the broken section lying in the canyon bottom, fifty feet below.

Somehow, though, the horse had scrambled on to firmer shelf and saved itself. But there was no way you could ever get an animal across again.

Frank was breathing hard. He kept eyeing the fissure over there while he got his wind back. He said, then, "Keep me covered, Drew," and walked out on the ledge.

It struck me then that he'd put on more weight with age than I'd thought. He took up a lot of the ledge width with his body bulk.

He reached the broken section and stopped. And then, before I could say a word, he turned his body to face the cliff, and began inching out with his boot toes.

After his first step with his left foot, there was no way he could step with his right. He had to shuffle along, his left forward, dragging up his right, leaning tight against the cliff face, his body twisted so that his chest scraped it, there being no shoulder room.

And then he came to a waist-high bulge in the cliff. He

stood there with sweat pouring off of him. I could see it glisten in the sunlight. He'd already lost his hat.

Right then we both knew he was a bit too thick in the belly, because when he tried to move he almost toppled backward.

I thought he was gone for sure. But somehow he regained his balance.

I'd heard Lola scream, and I knew then what I had to do.

"I can't make it, Drew," he called.

"I know it," I said. "Don't be a fool, Frank. Try to get back here."

Slowly then he began his retreat until he got back on wider footing. In another couple of minutes he was standing beside me, averting his eyes. "Hell to get old," he said.

I didn't wait for him to say anything else. I knew Lola was watching me.

I was slim enough, and I stepped out fast, before I could lose my nerve. I was to the narrow part and part way across it when he called, "For chrissake, be careful!"

I ignored him and kept moving, and got to the opening and looked in.

"It's a cave, all right," I called.

"Goddammit, boy!" he said. "You be careful, you hear?"

"Sure, Frank," I said, and I think I sounded a little sarcastic.

"I mean," he said, "he may be waiting in there for you."

"You trying to make me feel good?"

"I wish it was me, instead of you," he said.

And I could tell he meant it. "So do I," I said. I looked down into the canyon and I could see Lola looking up. I drew my Smith & Wesson then and stepped into the cave.

The fissure was high and narrow, with plenty of head-room. And after a few yards the ceiling rose even more to disappear into heavy shadow. Ahead of me the floor was hard and eroded smooth. I guessed that Frank was right when he suggested there might be another end to the cave up on top.

There was another thing. There was a pungent smell like that of ammonia.

I thought back to something I'd heard. Bat pee. Or bat guano. Or maybe a mixture of both, I couldn't remember which, gave off that odor. It made my skin crawl. Somewhere between me and the other end was a colony of bats.

There's something about bats that scares hell out of most people. And I was no exception.

I was wishing I had a miner's lamp.

I still had my pistol in my hand as I forced myself to edge forward into the increasing gloom. I was wondering what I'd do when I got into total blackness. Wondering also what Tolbert had done, if he had come this way.

Or if he had stopped and waited to ambush any damned fool like me who'd follow him in.

It did get pretty dark, but not pitch black like I expected. I could barely follow the cave bottom enough to keep moving, and I realized then that the opening up ahead couldn't be too far away.

At the darkest area I inched along, afraid I might step off into a bottomless hole. Instead I stepped into a sloppy mess that stunk to high heaven of ammonia, and I knew what I was wading in, all right. I looked up, and I could dimly make out what looked like a million little fox heads hanging upside down, and at that moment I came close to adding to the excrement.

Before I knew what I was doing. I was threshing my way, panicked, through the ungodly mess. When I felt dry ground underfoot I halted to get a grip on myself. It was less dark here. I looked back and up and saw I was beyond a low dropping arch that hid the bats, and I thought, Thank God that's done with!

And that's when a gun blasted out just ahead of me.

The noise it made in that cave was deafening. For a second I thought I was hit in the head, it hurt my ear drums so bad.

Then I saw the cloud of smoke drifting toward me, and like a damned fool I fired into it, and deafened myself for sure.

And that wasn't the worst of it.

The bats went insane. Inside of seconds they came swarming off the ceiling, and swept under the arch to engulf me.

I never could stand even the thought of being caught in a swarm of bats. All I could think of now was that they could carry rabies, and if I was bit or scratched by the sonsofbitches I might start foaming at the mouth. Then I remembered that down in Mexico they got some they call vampire bats that can suck the blood out of you.

The sonsofbitches were beating me with their wings as they fluttered around me. I lashed out wildly with both hands, still fisting my Smith & Wesson in my right. I hit plenty of them, they were that thick, and some of them fell at my feet, but most of them just kept going every which way around me.

I felt I was being cut and scratched whenever we made contact, and that I must be bleeding, and I expected that would draw them even more, like sharks do when they sense blood.

I'd been scared a few times in my life, but I never panicked like I did in the midst of those bats.

And then, for just a moment, I could see ahead in the dimness, through a brief clearing of the aroused swarm. What I glimpsed was Tolbert standing there just beyond.

He had his gun raised, and it blasted as I aimed and fired just as a goddamned bat came out of the swarm and struck my hand, and I knew I'd missed.

He didn't. The slug ripped through my shirt and laid a red hot branding iron across my right ribs. It took some muscle with it, I was sure, the way it hurt.

The two shots agitated the bats all over again, and this time I guess the concussion was too much for them. They swarmed toward the opening somewhere above and beyond

Tolbert, and I saw him duck, turn, and run just as the cloud of them obliterated my sight of him.

Much as I hated the repulsive critters, I guess they saved my life. I was hurting bad, but I was mad as hell, and I followed right behind them.

They flew up the sloping passage drilled out by the years of water torrents and right out into the sunlit sky. I didn't think bats ever did that. But maybe they were as panicked as I was, with all the shooting going on. Who the hell ever heard of men having a gunfight in a cave full of bats?

Tolbert must have scrambled up the slope ahead of them, because when they cleared out he was gone too.

I was getting weak from the loss of blood I could feel gushing from my wound, but I was still keyed up enough to keep going until I got to the top of the opening.

There was no more sight of the bats, wherever the hell they'd gone to. But I did catch sight of Tolbert. He was maybe a hundred yards up the escarpment and riding a pinto horse hard toward the summit.

If I'd had any doubt who he was, the pinto laid it to rest. I did wonder that he didn't wait around to see if he'd finished me off. But maybe he was spooked by the bats worse than I was.

After all, he was half Navajo and likely had their superstitions. Maybe there was some kind of a *chindi* about bats, too Whatever drove him, he rode without looking back.

Right now, I had other things to think about. Like getting back through that cave before I bled to death.

I half slid down the sloping chimney, staggered along the tunnel darkness, and was glad to eventually feel that bat crap under my boots again, because it meant I'd made it at least halfway.

I kept on and reached the entrance and came out into the daylight and slumped against the wall of the fissure. I was afraid to sit for fear I couldn't get up again. In front of me was the narrow ledge, and beyond was Frank standing there staring at me.

"Good God, boy!" he yelled. "What happened to you?"

I just shook my head.

"Sounded like shots in there," he called. "Dammit, boy, you're wounded!"

I didn't want to waste the strength to answer. Instead I forced myself out on the ledge, hoping I'd not collapse from weakness. If I did, there was that long drop to the canyon floor that would kill me.

I got to the narrow stretch and began working across it, stopping every few inches to rest, and eventually I made it.

Frank was waiting there to grab me and help me on to the talus. Once we got there, he said "Jeezus!"

I was so relieved to make it across that I felt almost cocky. I said, "What's the matter, Frank? A little blood bother you?" I knew my shirt was soaked with it.

"It ain't that, Drew. It's the smell. What the hell did you step in?"

"Bat crap," I said. I thought of something then. "You got to help me clean it off my boots before we go down to Lola."

He gave me a strange look, but all he said was, "Bats?"

"You ever in a gunfight in a cave of flying bats?" I said. "That's what Ike and I been doing in there."

"Ike?" he said. "In there? Did you get him, boy?"

"No," I said. "I missed. The goddamned bats were on his side."

"Tell me about it."

"Not now. Lola will want to hear about it too."

"I'll help you down."

"I want to get my boots clean first."

"Later, boy."

"No, goddamnit!" I said. *"Now!"*

It was all I could do to make it down that steep climb, even with Frank helping me.

Lola made no attempt to hide her concern, which might

have been a mistake. Despite the pain I was in I kept noticing Frank's face as he watched her strip off my shirt and finger softly the place where Tolbert's bullet had ploughed a furrow across my ribs.

Frank saw it wasn't a serious wound, although I'd lost some more blood on that sharp descent.

I'd just given them a quick rundown of what had happened.

"Dammit, Drew!" he said. "Right now when I need you, you got to get yourself shot up. I can't let Ike get away when we're so close."

"There's a mountainside between you and him now," I said. "You know you can't get a horse across that ledge like he did."

"We can get out of this canyon and go around and up the ridge and try to catch him. You up to that?"

I was lying there, liking the feel of Lola's fingers as she cleaned the wound with a frilly handkerchief she'd produced from somewhere and wet with water from a canteen.

"No, Frank," I said. "I'm hurting too bad for that."

He looked at me like he didn't want to accept that.

"I lost some blood," I said.

He looked at my shirt where Lola had tossed it aside. It was soaked with the stuff. "I can see that," he admitted.

"I'd just slow you up, even if I could make it," I said. "I'm sorry about that, Frank, damned sorry. You know how I feel."

That's when he glanced, frowning, at Lola and back at me. "I wish I did," he said. "I wish I did know for sure."

That kind of scared me a little, enough that I didn't express the suggestion I'd had in mind.

Right then, Lola did it for me. She did it casually enough.

She said, "Frank, you take Begay with you so you don't end up lost in this maze of canyons."

"I don't want to leave you here alone, Lola."

I said, "Hell, I can still shoot, Frank. I'm just not up to riding. Not just yet."

"All right," he said. "And Lola can shoot better than any of us." He hesitated, then said, "Drew, you take a short rest, then you and Lola follow around and up that ridge. You hear?"

Begay looked at me, and I could have swore he was about to grin about something.

"I hear, Frank," I said. "I'll be along shortly."

He said to Begay then, "We got to get up there to see where he goes."

A few minutes later they were riding down the canyon toward where the escarpments got lower and less steep.

Lola was trying to tie some kind of an improvised bandage over the crease wound, but there didn't seem to be any way she could make it stick. She kept fumbling around trying, though, and in spite of the hurt she tickled me.

"You've got a lot of muscles, Drew," she said. "All those young muscles!" She was holding the bandage in her right hand, and she reached up with her left and kneaded my shoulder. I liked that.

She reached up further then, and stroked my cheek. Then she leaned close and kissed me. She was breathing hard. "Oh, God!" she said.

That did it. I forgot I was hurting and grabbed her in my arms. That was a mistake, because I felt like I'd just been shot again. I let go when the pain struck. But she didn't. She had both her arms around me now and was squeezing.

Well, I've heard tell of pleasurable pain, but as far as I'm concerned, they don't mix. Pleasure and pain, I mean.

"Ease up, godammit!" I said.

She did, but only a little. "Better?" she said.

"Yeah, some." I was holding her loosely now, still hurting but not ready to get free.

We just lay there a while, neither of us moving, and my mind got off my wound and began to think of other things.

She kissed me a couple of times more, and rubbed her smooth cheek against my scuffy jowl. I was wishing I'd shaved.

Well, if I hadn't been weak from loss of blood I know what I'd have done then. But the weakness was coming back, and I knew I wasn't going to be able to do what I wanted to do.

She could feel that too, by then, and she began to pull away from me. Pretty soon we were apart, and I was lying there alone, and she was sitting up and just staring down at me.

At first I couldn't bring myself to meet her eyes, I was so ashamed. Not of what I'd wanted to do. Of what I wasn't capable of doing.

I met her stare finally, and there wasn't any resentment there. Just a sort of resigned look. As if my incapacity was nothing new to her. It made me wonder about her and Frank.

"I'm sorry," I said. "I lost too much blood."

"I understand," she said. "It was the wrong time, Drew."

I felt better then, the way she said it. It sounded like a promise.

CHAPTER 11

PART of it was my embarrassment, I guess, and part of it was that being there alone with her I began to worry about another bunch of Navajos coming up the canyon looking for us.

They'd be out to kill for sure if they'd found those bodies lying down there where Buck Ardmore had dropped them.

Lola was watching me, and I guess she saw my growing concern. But she misinterpreted it.

She smiled and said, "Don't worry about it, Drew. It'll come back to you, when the hurting stops."

"That wasn't what I was thinking about," I said. "The thought occurs that this isn't the safest spot to be."

"You told Frank you couldn't ride yet."

"Yeah, well, I was lying a little."

"I guessed that," she said. She paused. "You think you can follow them now?"

"I think so. I wonder that Frank didn't insist on it."

She hesitated, then said, "Sometimes I wonder how much he cares for me."

I should have kept my mouth shut, but I couldn't. Not when I knew Frank better than that.

I said, "He cares, Lola. I know he cares." I paused. "Maybe that's part of the reason why—I mean, maybe it all wasn't because I'm wounded."

She gave me a sudden cool appraisal. "Don't go getting noble on me, Drew. Not now, after we were that close to it."

"Noble? No, I guess not. But, still, he's always been a hero to me. A thing like that is hard to shake off."

Her manner was abruptly cold as ice. And so was her voice. "Are we leaving or not?"

"We're leaving," I said.

Without another word, she began gathering up our gear.

We mounted up and rode down out of the canyon, and the silence held between us. I couldn't figure out why she was acting so different. But, like most young cowboys, my experience with women was pretty limited.

I didn't bother to look for Frank and Begay's tracks at first. My ribs were hurting too bad, and they had to follow the canyon bottom.

It wasn't until we got close to where the Navvy bodies still lay, being feasted on by a flock of buzzards, that I began looking off to our right, away from them, and I picked up the trail.

The sight of the corpses being eaten was too much for Lola. "Oh, God!" she said. "We should have buried them."

I knew that Begay would give them a wide berth, and that's how I stumbled onto his tracks so easily. He'd crowded to the north edge of the canyon, and all we had to do was follow it as it lowered to become a sloping shoulder.

I gave no more thought to the bodies or the buzzards. My mind now was occupied with thinking that the slope ahead was the bottom of the long ridge that I'd seen Tolbert riding up as he fled the bat cave.

Up there somewhere, where the ridge became part of the sacred mountain, there could be a showdown if Frank and he confronted each other.

In spite of the pain I was feeling, I had an overpowering desire to be there if it happened. And a sudden concern for Frank. I wasn't exactly sure whose side Begay would take, the more I thought about it. I began to regret I'd given him that carbine.

I kicked heels to my horse. Lola gigged up beside me, leading the pack animal along. Her coldness was gone now. I could sense the excitement growing in her.

"You expecting something, Drew?"

"Not necessarily," I said. "But if there is something, I want to be there."

"Me too," she said. "Drew, can you handle your gun?"

My whole side was stiff now with soreness, and it hurt even more to raise my arm, but I said, "I'll handle it."

I sounded more confident than I felt.

We followed the tracks of Frank and Begay up the slope to where they entered a broad expanse of junipers. They went through a section that was pretty thick, and when they came out again, there were only those of one horse, which I judged to be Frank's.

Someplace in there Begay must have turned off into the foliage and deserted him.

I began to swear.

"What's wrong?" Lola said.

I told her, and she shocked me by swearing too.

"That no-good Navajo bum!" she said. "He was just waiting his chance!"

I think she was mad mostly because she'd failed to con him into staying, rather than because he'd left Frank to go it alone.

"Might be just as well," I said. "In a showdown he might have turned against Frank."

She thought about that as we followed Frank's trail.

"Maybe you're right," she said finally. "Provided he didn't runoff to join up with Tolbert."

"Not likely," I said. "Not with the judge's *chindi* trying to find Ike."

"I was forgetting about that."

"You can bet Begay hasn't. He may pretend to scoff some at the Navvy superstitions, but deep down he believes as strong as the rest of them. You saw how he backed away from offering to bury those Navvies Ardmore killed."

"That was a terrible thing Ardmore did," she said. "I never liked him. Frank says he's a killer by nature."

"I can believe it."

She shuddered. "The way he picked them off in cold blood!" She hesitated, then said, "Where do you think he is now?"

"Begay?"

"Buck Ardmore."

"Not far," I said. "He's out to keep an eye on Frank until Frank finds Tolbert."

"That may be soon!"

It could be damned soon, I thought. It could be right ahead of us. I was suddenly torn between wanting to hurry and a need to be cautious. Again I was worried about Lola being in danger. It was damned foolish for Frank to take her on a manhunt. That was driven home to me now that we were in the danger zone, even if I hadn't thought too much about it in the beginning. Then, I guess, I had just been glad she'd be close to me, where I could see her all the time and maybe touch her once in a while. But now things were different.

I kept wondering about what Frank had said back there in Staffold, about having her along because she was an expert rifle shot. She hadn't aimed at all against those Navvies when they accosted us.

Had she shot someone on earlier manhunts with Frank? I wondered. I asked her straight out.

"I don't want to talk about it," she said.

"You weren't about to use that rifle when those Indians had us cornered," I said.

"The Navajos aren't warlike Indians, Drew. They've been civilized for years."

"That's what I read," I said. "But about the ones in these canyons, I'm not so sure." I paused. "But what I'm asking is, I think, do you have the stomach to shoot a man if it's necessary? Have you ever done it?"

She didn't answer me.

I kept on. "Did you?"

"Leave me alone, Drew. I said I don't want to talk about it."

So there I was. I knew if I pressed any harder she'd get mad at me, and I didn't want that to happen. But her refusal was something to think about. Something could have happened in the past that she found hard to live with.

I put it out of my mind. I had to think of what was ahead, not behind.

The terrain here was rocky and mostly bare except for the spots of juniper and, as we climbed, some piñon. At the higher reaches we could see the mountain slope covered with a fringe of pines. The top was still a long way off.

Frank's trail sign, where I could pick it out between expanses of bare rock, showed he was continuing upward. There wasn't any other way he could go, because the scarp wasn't much more than a sharp ridge.

I figured that Tolbert had a considerable lead, if he'd kept running from the time I'd last seen him. He'd had time to reach the summit and pass beyond, if that was his intention.

He also could be waiting up there in ambush. He'd have a big advantage then.

I was slightly stunned at my next thought. Maybe Ike didn't want to kill Ladd.

But why?

I must have shaken my head, not knowing the answer.

Because Lola said, "What's on your mind, Drew?"

I told her.

"It may well be," she said. "You know, Frank once told me how he pleaded in court during Tolbert's trial. How he asked that some leniency be shown because of Ike's treatment at the hands of those thugs claiming to represent the railroad."

"Then he's always felt some regret about bringing Ike in, considering the sentence that was given him?"

"I'm sure of it."

"Even if it did give him the start of a big reputation?"

"Even so," she said.

"But now he's out to get Ike again."

She was quiet for a moment, then she said, almost reluctantly, "Don't you know why, Drew? Because of me."

Well, I knew that. Frank had as much as told me back in Staffold. I didn't know what to say, so I kept my mouth shut.

"You know then?"

I nodded.

"God forgive me," she said. "What we are driven to do for money!"

I glanced at her face, and I could see a kind of pain there. But it was pain mixed with determination. She'd see it through, if she could. She'd see that Frank took Tolbert again or got killed trying.

That chilled me. But—God help *me!*—it excited me too.

We kept plodding along as the ridge broadened into an actual shoulder, and eventually we reached the spot from where I'd last seen Tolbert, the place where I'd come out of the bat cave chimney. We weren't even halfway to the summit here.

The tracks went right on past, only now there were those of Tolbert too, and we followed them. The climb was steep, and we had to halt again and again to rest the animals. And me too. The sun beat down fiercely; it seemed even hotter in these high reaches than it had been down in the canyons.

Eventually we reached a stand of ponderosa pine, and rode into the shade gratefully.

"I wonder where Ike is leading him," Lola said.

I had reached the point, with my wound, that I didn't care. I was ready to give up and make camp right there among those ponderosas, and stay.

I told her as much.

"You can't, Drew," she said. "We've got to follow. Frank may need help."

"Dammit!" I said. "I'm half dead. Can't you see that?" It was the first time I'd ever spoken cross to her like that. But I was near the edge.

"I'll go on alone, then," she said.

"Chrissakes, Lola, have a heart, will you?"

"Of course, Drew," she said sweetly. "You stay here and rest up. You can follow when you feel better."

"Go ahead, then!" I said wildly.

She took the pack mule and rode on up the mountain.

I lay down, stretched out, and tried to relax, but I couldn't. Five minutes later I hauled myself back into the saddle and was riding after her.

Just about the time I was wondering how I'd overtake her, I saw her about two hundred yards ahead, waiting for me.

I cussed long and bitterly to myself, calling myself a damned fool in every way I could, before I reached her.

"Drew, you really shouldn't," she said.

I rode right by her without saying a word.

Out of the corner of my eye I could see her smiling faintly. That made me madder than ever. But I was too exhausted and pain-filled to make an issue of it.

As if to make some amends, she said, "You're a very tough man, Drew. And I admire you for it."

I knew what she was up to, of course. Still, her words made me sit up straighter in my saddle. That only made my pain worse, but I stayed that way, knowing she was watching.

And just about then is when a gun battle opened up somewhere near the summit.

"Drew!" she said.

"I hear. Frank must have caught up with Ike!"

"Don't let me down now, Drew!" she called. It was over her shoulder, because she was driving her mount up the slope, fit to kill it.

She was gone from my sight before I could get going, disappearing into some trees. The last glimpse I had of her, she was was reaching for that Winchester of hers, then thinking better of it, I guess, because she withdrew her hand.

But she'd be drawing it from the scabbard when she got above, I knew. Especially if Frank was in danger. Her loyalty toward him was fierce, I thought. Or was it only the money? His being the means to gaining the bounty offered on Tolbert? I thrust that thought from my mind at once. It made me sick that I could even think such a thing about her.

I followed as best I could, but didn't sight her again.

There had been two rifles blasting away, by the sound of it. Then silence. A dread seeped into me. Don't let it be Lola, I kept thinking. Whatever happened up there, don't let it be Lola.

I don't know how I made it to the top as fast as I did, the way I was hurting. As I got higher the pines gave way to ground juniper, a few stunted aspens, and some white firs, and I was straining to see what happened.

I stopped in the fringe of wind-stunted growth just as another exchange of shots took place. All I could tell at first was that a duel was being fought from opposite sides of the broad, nearly-flat summit. The bullets were flying back and forth.

Lola startled me by appearing suddenly beside me. She had dismounted somewhere in the foliage. I glanced at her and saw she had her Winchester in her hands.

She said, "Who? Frank and Tolbert?"

"Or Begay. Or Ardmore," I said.

"We've got to help him!" she cried.

I could see she was worked up about Frank being in danger. It was the first time I'd ever seen her really excited. Out of control nearly. I should have known right then that there was still a lot of something between them.

I was nerved up myself, not being experienced in combat. And my wound was hurting badly. But at the same time I felt I had to show some manhood in front of her or she wouldn't think much of me.

I scanned the east rim from where the last shots had come, and it seemed to me that over there was where Frank would be. I said, "Frank's to the east there, I think." It was a wild guess I was to regret.

Because just then was when the other rifleman rose slightly at the north edge of the flat, his head turned to the east where his target was.

Lola must have seen him too, because she said, "Begay!" and fired.

She missed as Begay dropped back. She put a couple of fast shots into the scrub brush that hid him, and we heard the bullets whine off some rocks behind the screen. He must have had good cover there.

Only he did a peculiar thing then. He raised a hand and waved it back and forth in our direction.

Keyed up as she was, Lola snapped off another shot without thinking. The hand turned red and disappeared.

That was one of her trick shots for you.

Frank, on the east rim, opposite us, saw what she'd done, I guess, because he raised up for a better look.

Only it wasn't Frank, it was Ardmore.

"Hold your fire, goddammit!" I said to her. "Frank isn't in this! It's between Begay and Buck."

"Oh, God!" she said. "Did I do wrong?"

I didn't answer her.

"Why are they fighting?" There was near hysteria in her voice.

"Maybe Begay couldn't forget how Buck killed those Navajos in the canyon."

"I thought he was shooting at Frank!" She sounded ready to cry. "Oh, God!"

"It wasn't your fault," I said.

"But it was. It was!"

What could I say to that?

Ardmore, seeing Begay wounded, raced to take advantage of it. From our own position I could glimpse him a couple of times as he moved toward Begay's, making his way from cover to cover.

I had half a notion to shoot the sonofabitch, but I kept

thinking back and feeling it likely enough that he'd saved our own lives from those canyon Navvies. Besides, I wasn't a killer. Not yet, anyway.

Lola saw him too, but she didn't raise her weapon again. What she'd done to Begay seemed to have taken all the sap out of her.

I was deeply concerned about what was coming next. My sympathy was with Begay, but it appeared he had gone after Ardmore and attacked him. That gave Buck the right to defend himself. And it was clear that Buck was out now to get him.

I was still wondering what to do when we heard a shot and Begay came staggering backward out of his cover and fell against a jutting boulder and lay still.

Ardmore appeared briefly and gave him a glance to see if he was dead. Even from where we were watching, we could see the blood running out of a hole in Begay's head. I swear I saw Ardmore grin before he disappeared back in the brush.

He was a killer, all right. A normal man can't smile after he kills, at least that was my belief.

I hesitated, half-expecting him to seek us out. When he didn't, I edged out cautiously toward where Begay lay, flinging glances here and there around the summit.

Lola was right on my heels, as if she needed me for support as we neared the Navvy's body. I could imagine how she felt.

We reached him and stood there looking down at the way he was sprawled against that rock outcrop.

"He's shot through the head," Lola said, her voice breaking.

It was then I thought I saw his chest moving.

I dropped down beside him and touched him above his left temple, and my fingers came away covered with blood. I said, "Shot *in* the head. But not through."

Ardmore's bullet had ploughed a crease across his skull that dropped him. If that wasn't enough to keep him unconscious, there was a bump the size of an egg on the other side where he'd struck the rock as he fell.

Lola was on her knees beside me now. "He's breathing!"

"I know."

She reached for his bloodied right hand and lifted it, and we could see where she'd shot off the first joint of his trigger finger. A wild moan escape her. "My fault, my fault!"

"Dammit! Don't make over him! If Ardmore's watching he'll finish him off for sure."

She dropped the hand as if it was hot. "I'll kill Ardmore first," she said. And there was sudden iron in her voice.

"I'm going to the rim and see if I can see where he went," I said. "Get into those rocks till I get back."

She hesitated, then crawled into cover. She seemed reluctant to leave the Navvy's side.

I made my way to the east rim, from where Buck had done most of his shooting. Right away I saw him part way down a shoulder that led to a ridge above another canyon. He was leading his horse, and not looking back.

The canyon, like all those we'd seen, rayed out from the mountain hub. This one, though, extended to a distant vast desert valley, dotted with sandstone buttes like monuments that made it look like a graveyard for giants. It seemed to extend forever until it was lost in horizon haze.

I went back to where Lola waited.

"He's gone."

"After Frank?"

"Who else?"

At that moment Begay groaned and stirred.

She was beside him instantly.

Her concern irked me, I don't know why. After all, she was only acting womanly, I guess. I suppose I was resenting her lack of sympathy for my own wound when she forced me to keep going up the mountain because of Frank's danger.

Begay suddenly sat up. He had a wild look in his eyes, and they went to my old carbine lying where he'd dropped it.

"None of that," I said. "You're among friends, now."

His eyes steadied on mine for a moment before shifting to Lola.

She reached for his wounded hand again, and he held it out to her. She took his wrist gently, and her face went pale as she stared at his missing finger.

It was bleeding badly. She jerked her blouse loose from her waistband, and tugged it around so she could hold it over the stump. "I'm sorry," she said softly. "So very sorry."

"I try to show you truce," he said weakly. "But I don't have flag to wave."

"I shouldn't have shot," she said.

He didn't say anything to that. He was a shrewd Indian, I thought. He knew he had her deep in his debt now. He'd take advantage of it if he could.

"Take a knife and cut off some of my shirttail," Lola said to me. "We've got to make bandages."

I took out a pocket knife and managed to cut some cloth strips for her.

We must have spent a half hour getting his wounds compressed and wrapped and the bleeding slowed.

Through it all he didn't whimper. He was one tough sonofabitch when it came to tolerating pain. He was tougher than I was in that respect. But then, what the hell, Indians are brought up that way.

What bothered me now was thinking back to how I'd moaned and groaned a little about my own hurt. The damned Navvy was making me look bad by comparison.

I said brusquely, "Why the hell did Frank leave the summit? Now he's got to catch up."

"Can you go on?" Lola said. She didn't look up from finishing her dressing of Begay's wounds.

She knew damned well I had to say yes. I couldn't let her and Begay go off alone together, that I was sure.

"Let's go," I said.

And at that moment Frank burst in on us.

We were so surprised we just stared.

"I heard the shooting," he said. "I was part way down, trying for a better look of where Ike was going."

"Did you see Ardmore? He was behind you."

"No. The bastard must have hid, and I wasn't looking. I came back up fast when I heard the shots. What happened here?"

I gave him a quick rundown.

He said to Begay, "Can you ride?"

"Yes, Hosteen."

"I thought you deserted me."

Begay didn't answer.

"He was out to get Ardmore," I said.

"Let's go then," Frank said.

We started down the eastern slope of the mountain, and we got near the bottom without ever seeing Ardmore again.

And there ahead of us was that enormous cemetery for giants. A vast sage-covered valley spotted with huge, natural monuments of reddish sandstone.

They damned well could be our own tombstones, I thought.

It had been dry and hot even on top of the mountain, but here the air off that desert graveyard hit us in the face like it was from a blast furnace.

Frank reined up and was quiet, staring out there, now that Tolbert was gone from sight.

I thought of thirst, and said, "How are we fixed for water?"

"I've got only a half canteen left," Lola said.

"Mine's full," Frank said. "Begay showed me a spring coming up the mountain." He paused. "Before he deserted me."

"Mine's half gone," I said. "Yours full, Begay?"

He tapped the canteen hanging from his saddle. There was a bullet hole in it. "Empty," he said.

"That valley out there looks very dry," Lola said.

"Any springs there, Begay?"

"They there," he said. "But I don't been there since I was a kid."

CHAPTER 12

OUT on that desert filled with monuments Tolbert was on the run, and we were chasing him. Where Ardmore was now we didn't know.

We weren't in the best of shape for a desert chase, what with a shot-up Navajo guide and a rib-wounded and sorely hurting young white. But we had a determined Frank Ladd and a determined Lola.

Right about then I was wondering if we'd ever get across that desert expanse, let alone catch up with Tolbert.

And where was Ardmore? Would he open up, sight unseen, on Begay? We still needed the guide, whether or not he remembered the valley.

I realized then how much I leaned on Ladd, relying on him to make the decisions.

Without his presence I'd have felt responsible for Lola's safety, growing out of my desire for her. The desire was nothing new to me. The sense of responsibility would have been.

It was late afternoon now, and Frank sat his horse, still staring over the valley as if he could see Tolbert out there.

He said, "Begay, we'll make camp below. I'll be down shortly."

"Yes, Hosteen," Begay said.

He led the way down to the flat and picked a tolerable spot to camp.

He spoke to Lola, not me. "We stay here tonight, I think." Then he added a word or two in Navajo.

I said, sharply, "What did you call her?"

He grinned at my tone. "It mean beautiful woman."

I didn't like that at all. "Watch what you say!"

"Is beautiful, don't she?"

Lola laughed, and I turned to find her eyes on me.

"Answer the question, Drew," she said.

"He's got no right to say that to you."

"I don't mind. Every woman likes a compliment."

"It's more than that," I said. "Dammit, it's how he feels!"

"Even so," she said. "It's still a compliment."

"To be lusted after by an Indian?"

"Sure," she said. "Why not?"

"Goddammit, Lola, that ain't right!"

All she did was laugh at me, and that made me madder than ever. But I was too beat to argue about it.

I suppose Begay was too. Neither one of us was in shape to do much about making camp or taking care of the horses. Once dismounted, we had to leave that to her.

That didn't seem to bother Begay at all, but it did me. No doubt he was accustomed to squaws doing most of the menial work, but I wasn't.

It was a dry camp, and I said irritably, "Couldn't you find us a spring somewhere?"

"I told you, I don't been here."

"Then you don't know where we're going?"

"I think Tolbert know."

"Does he? He didn't get as much help so far as he figured, I'm thinking."

"Like I tell you, because most Navajos afraid of *chindi*." He paused. "But they die to try to help, back in canyon."

"That why you tried to kill Ardmore?"

He nodded. "Those men he kill, they same clan as me."

I understood then. A clan among the Navvies was like an extended family.

The next morning we had only a quarter canteen of water each between Lola and me. I said to Begay, "First thing, you better find us a water hole."

"How much time we can waste?"

"We can't waste any."

"Better we go then."

"That's a desert ahead."

"No is a desert."

Frank was listening.

"What do you mean?" I said.

"To a *belecana*, is desert, maybe. To the Dinéh, no."

"There are some of your people out there?" Frank said.

"Maybe fifty families, Hosteen. I don't been there, but I hear. When Kit Carson come, one young chief name Hoskinini lead some people there, they say. Soldiers chase. He lead his people to San Juan River near rock name Mexican Hat. It look like hat Mexicans wear. Dinéh cross river, then water come high. Soldiers don't can cross, go back to fort."

"That was fifty years ago," I said.

"Hoskinini bring people back across the river then, because other side Ute land, and Utes our enemy. Hoskinini and his people they still here, with children and children's children."

"So there's water out there?" Frank said.

"Got to be, eh, Hosteen?" He paused. "Old chief Hoskinini still live there someplace."

"Still alive?"

"They say."

"Would he help Tolbert?"

"Who know? He don't help, maybe Tolbert last chance, I think."

"What about *chindi*?" I said.

He shrugged. "Old Hoskinini, maybe he remember those bad time against *belecanas*. Time when *he* have to run. So maybe he help Tolbert."

"*Chindi* or no *chindi*?" I said.

"Maybe, I think." He paused. "I find water out there, Hosteen."

"I hope so. We've got to think about her," I said, nodding toward Lola. I was somewhat relieved at what he'd said.

"Sure, I know. I been think about her," he said.

My relief left me.

As we rode, Begay seemed thoughtful. Finally, he said, "I think about Hoskinini. I sure he help Tolbert."

"What makes you sure?"

"I remember something I hear. Long time ago, maybe thirty, thirty-five year, Hoskinini he, like now, chief of all this north country. These Dinéh still warriors, hate whites. They listen nobody but Hoskinini. No whites bother him or his people for many year. Whites don't bother because Navajos don't raid south. Only sometimes raid north against Utes."

We all listened, waiting for him to go on.

"Then a thing happen. Two white-eyes come. Prospectors. They look for silver. In this valley."

I'd read something about two prospectors being killed back around 1880. "Hoskinini killed them?" I said.

"No, not him. They killed by some Paiutes Hoskinini let live here. Still, no soldiers come."

"So?"

"Maybe four, five year pass. Then two more prospector killed. This time by Navajos, they say. Soldiers come, can't find who done killing. So they take Hoskinini. Take him to Fort Wingate, throw him in jail. They keep him in jail one year." Begay paused, then said, "He don't ever forget, I think."

I saw his point then. Having been in a cell for a year, the old chief would remember the hell he'd gone through. He'd sympathize with Tolbert's worse hell, twenty years as long. He'd not want to see Ike captured to await a hanging.

All this didn't make me any easier in my mind. If that desert of monuments wasn't scary enough, the threat of a revenge-minded chief and his renegades was.

Worse than that maybe, we might be riding right into their clutches.

Lola had been listening too, and I could see her struck by the same concern. She said, "Would he hurt us?"

Begay only shrugged.

I said to him, "You ever meet the chief?"

He shook his head. "I only see one time. But he is hero to my people."

"If we run into him, maybe you can talk to him."

He looked shocked. "Me? No, no! He most powerful man in north country! He don't talk to me."

"You don't know that."

"I know, all right." He looked scared. "Maybe he kill me because I with you. He live like in old time. No *belecanas* allowed."

We were deep into that valley of monuments now, and I never saw anything like it. Up close those sandstone buttes were unbelievable, some of them rising from a sage and sparse-grassed floor to heights of hundreds of feet.

"They're beautiful!" Lola said.

A little while earlier I would have agreed with her. Now I wasn't so sure. "If what Begay tells us is true," I said, "they can be deadly too." Right about then I was seeing a bunch of hostiles behind every butte.

I said, "We've still got the other problem. Water."

"There water here," Begay said. "Hoskinini people, they got to drink too."

"Find it then!" Frank said. "I'm saving what I've got."

"I find," he said. "Pretty soon."

"You damn well better."

Like I said, it was hotter than a furnace in that valley. Lola and I both sipped from our canteens when our thirst got unbearable. Each time, she offered hers to Begay, but he smiled at her and shook his head.

I could tell she wanted badly to make some amends for what she'd done to his hand. I could also tell that an Indian, a Navajo at least, can survive better without water than a white man.

I kept thinking about Tolbert now. I could visualize him seeking out the powerful old chief and saying, "I come to you, Grandfather, because there is no hope for me else-where."

Grandfather was a term of address Navajo men used com-monly among themselves, regardless of kin. In this case it would be one of respect.

It would be hard for the chief to turn down his plea for protection, I was thinking.

Begay did find water for us soon. It was in a wash near the base of a lesser butte. The dusty green of a few straggly cottonwoods was what caught his eye, I guess. They weren't much to see, but in that harsh land they stood out like a piece of the Garden of Eden.

There were wild animal tracks and old sheep droppings all around, which meant that Begay was right about the valley being inhabited. What little graze had been in that area was gone now, and the sheep had moved on. In sparse country like this, the Navvies would have to keep their herds grazing far and wide to find grass.

I whittled a plug from a cottonwood branch to plug the bullet hole in Begay's canteen, since his right hand was still useless.

The spring at this time of year was hardly more than a trickle, and it took a while to fill our canteens and horses but we were in good shape when we left.

I felt a lot better. I realized that the previous night's rest had strengthened me, although my ribs were still stiff and sore, and when I stretched to reach anything the skin felt like it was being ripped off of me.

Begay, with that crease on his skull and the swollen bruise on the other side of his head, must have had a headache at least, but he didn't complain. Worse yet must have been the agony of his shot-off finger. It made me wince just to think about it. Although it was wrapped in the bandage Lola had fashioned, I noticed he favored it gingerly.

Lola kept eyeing it from time to time, and when I caught her doing so I could see she was close to tears.

And when Begay met her glance, she'd show her remorse and her sympathy. At such times he'd smile faintly, as if he forgave her for what she'd done to him.

Such is the hold of a good-looking woman, I thought. God help us men! I wouldn't have expected such feeling from an Indian. But then, how many had I known? Did they treat their squaws with such forbearance? I had my doubts of that.

From the spring a kind of trail had led eastward, and Begay picked out Tolbert's tracks despite a confusion of hoofprints.

All we had to do for a while was watch out that none of them left the trail, and we relied on Begay for that.

"How far ahead is he?" I said.

"Not far. And Navajo killer right behind him."

He'd taken to calling Admore by that name.

"Ardmore!" Frank said. "How did he get ahead?"

"Last night, I think," Begay said.

"You knew it all the time," I said.

He didn't answer me, but he didn't deny it either.

"And Tolbert is close?" Frank said. "Goddammit, Begay! He could beat us out of that reward!"

"I think Tolbert find Hoskinini first."

"And maybe he won't!"

It was noon of the next day when we found out for sure. We were just passing a high sandstone spire when we heard rifle-fire from maybe a mile away.

Begay said, "Other side next butte, I think."

There was a half mile of open space between us and the shooting.

Frank said, "Wait here. Stay hid." He rode ahead.

I waited a few minutes, and I saw Lola giving me a critical eye, and I couldn't stand it any longer. I got up and started to ride.

"I'm going with you," she said.

"No!" I said. "Not till I see what's going on." I could see she was going to argue, and I softened my tone. "One rider can sneak over there. More than one and we'd likely be seen." Which didn't make any sense when you thought about it, but I took off alone before she could protest further.

Begay started to follow, but I waved him back. "Stay with her!" What good could he do me, with his trigger finger shot away? And if worse came to worst, he could at least lead her out of this wild north country. And with his hand being wounded I figured she could repel any advances he might try to make.

As I got closer I skirted around to the south, keeping close to the talus base. The firing was all on the eastern side.

As I rounded the fragments of fallen sandstone, I saw, directly ahead, separated by only a few yards and fighting side by side, Frank and Buck Ardmore. They were so intent on battle that neither noticed my approach.

I was afraid to announce my presence. I knew instinctively that a man in combat must be hair-triggered high, and might whirl and put a bullet into me on pure reflex.

I waited for a brief lull in the firing before I called out, and it was almost fatal.

Ardmore did whirl and shoot, just as I dropped as much from fright as instinct.

"Hold it!" Frank yelled.

"Sonofabitch!" Ardmore snarled.

I looked up and he was staring at me with those pale eyes of his and looking mad as hell.

"You goddam fool!" he said.

That made *me* mad. "You spooky bastard!" I yelled. "Don't you look before you shoot?"

"Not in a firefight, I don't. What the hell you mean sneaking up like that?"

I could see he was shaken by how close he'd come to making a mistake, and that eased my anger a little. I ignored him and spoke to Frank. "Who're you fighting?"

"Injuns is all I know. I come around the butte here and they opened up on *me*, as well as Buck. Buck fought them off till I got into cover here," Frank said. "Lucky for me he did too."

"This old man rode right into a noisy ambush," Ardmore said. "Lucky those goddam Navvies are poor shots."

"You're sure?"

"We're alive yet, aren't we?"

"I mean, are you sure they're Navvies?"

"They are, all right," Frank said. "Where's Lola?"

"Back at that last butte," I said.

That smart bastard Ardmore said, "What do you think we've been shooting at?"

That's when a sniper opened up on us from the butte top three hundred feet above. He was wearing a red headband instead of a hat. How he got up there I couldn't imagine, unless there was some kind of ascent possible on the other side.

He was shooting at us from the rim of what had been a plateau a million years ago, except that erosion had rounded off the top to a kind of shallow dome. He was lying prone on the very edge, sighting down at us.

The scary part, aside from his bullets, was to see the way the dome made his feet higher than his head, so that he looked like he might come sliding headfirst off of there any second. He had guts, I'll say that for him.

We cringed down in the rocks, but there was no way we could get into adequate cover. My own carbine was still on my horse, but Frank rolled onto his back and snapped a shot upward and missed. The Indian fired back and put a bullet through Frank's hat where it had fallen from his head when he rolled.

Then Buck flipped himself over and fired.

I had my head twisted to see the Indian, and I saw him lose his grasp on his rifle and try to wriggle backward. But his movement started him sliding forward.

He howled as he skidded off. He didn't even turn over, just

kept diving headfirst until he struck the rocks high on the talus, splattering brains and blood all over them.

"Now," Ardmore said, "there's a *good* Indian."

I felt a little sick, myself. But, after all, the Navvy had been trying to kill us. I said, "How many Navvies are out there?"

"Must be a dozen at least," Frank said. "If we had Begay, maybe we could parley."

I looked at Ardmore, and wondered what he'd do if he knew we had Begay back. I was thinking that if I brought Begay over, Ardmore might shoot him on sight.

The other Navajos must have seen their sniper fall, because they began shooting again. Bullets were whanging off the rocks around us, and it seemed to me there was an army out there. I'd never been under fire like that before.

From my cover I called out to Ardmore, "You want to parley?"

I could see him from my position, and he didn't look as cocky as he had before. He didn't answer me, but he appeared to be thinking about it.

Frank was closer to me, and he said, "We're dead if we don't. Only a matter of time. I wonder if any of them Injuns can speak English?"

I said then, "Do you want me to go and get Begay? He's with Lola."

Ardmore must have overheard. He said, "The hell! I thought I killed the bastard." He was all interest now.

The trouble was, I didn't like his show of interest.

"Bring him in," Frank said. "But leave Lola back there."

"Not unless I can be sure Buck won't shoot him," I said. "They had their own shootout back there on the mountain."

I was watching Buck's face as close as I could with lead ricocheting around. I couldn't tell much because he was peering out of cover, looking for a target.

He said, suddenly, loud enough for Frank to hear, "Wasn't me started that fracas. It was the damned Indian that tried to drygulch *me*. I don't figure to give him another chance like that."

"I can bring him in unarmed," I said. "He isn't any danger to you now. His hand's all bandaged, and his trigger finger is shot off."

Ardmore scowled. "I thought I shot him in the head!"

"Go get him, Drew," Frank said. "We got to have somebody can talk to these Navvies in their own lingo."

"Buck?" I said.

Buck nodded. "Go get him. We need the red bastard. But if he makes one move against me he'll have a missing head as well as a finger."

Frank was stripping off his shirt. He tied it to his carbine barrel and lifted it up and waved it kind of uncertainly. Some buck shot a hole through the shirt, and then everything got quiet.

"Get going!" he said to me. "But leave Lola hid back there, you hear?"

"What about Buck?" I said. "Do we have his word?"

"Yeah, you got it," Buck said.

The trouble was, I didn't know if his word was good.

But I began slipping my way back to where my horse was sheltered. I swung onto him fast and put him into a run for the other butte, half-expecting a bullet to catch me or the horse, but nothing happened.

Lola and Begay were still there, waiting.

"Is Frank all right?" she said, first thing.

"So far," I said, and briefly explained what was happening, and what we wanted.

As I expected, Begay objected. "You think I be stupid?" he said.

I knew then I'd made a mistake in mentioning that Ardmore was there with Frank.

"Ardmore says you attacked him—it wasn't his doing," I said.

"Sure, I do," Begay said.

"You can't trust Ardmore," Lola said.

"Listen, Lola, Frank is there. Keep that in mind. And a parley is his only chance. Ours, too, probably."

"Then I'm coming along," she said.

"Begay?" I said.

He was a long time answering. Then, finally, he said, "She go, I go."

So that's the way it was with him, I guess.

CHAPTER 13

WHEN we got back to where I'd left Frank and Ardmore, there were a couple of the Navajos a short distance away, half-hidden in the talus.

"What's happened so far?" I said.

"Been some hollering back and forth, but none of them understand English," Frank said. "But I guess they know we want to talk."

He turned to Begay, and said, "You willing?"

Begay hadn't taken his eyes off Ardmore. Ardmore hadn't taken his off Begay either, even though he could see his hand was bandaged.

Without shifting his glance, Begay said, "What you want I do, Hosteen?"

"I want to talk to their leader," Frank said. He saw the way Ardmore was staring at the guide. "Buck, if you mess with Begay, I'll kill you myself."

Ardmore said, "You could only try, old man."

"Just remember," Frank said, "that him talking can save your own neck. Can you get that through your head?"

"All right," Buck said. "Let him have at it."

Frank motioned Begay up beside him. "Tell them what I told you."

Begay called out so that the waiting Navajos could hear. One of them answered in their language.

Begay said, "They say Hoskinini their leader. You want to talk, you leave all guns and come out."

"Like hell," Ardmore said.

Frank said, "Buck, you do what you want. I'm going out. And the others with me. Stay alone here and see how long you can last." He looked at Lola. "Dammit! Lola, you shouldn't have come."

"I had to be with you, Frank," she said.

"I don't trust the red bastards," Buck said.

"Your choice." Frank stood up and made a show of laying down his weapons. He gestured to us, and we followed, except Buck, me dropping my gun belt and pistol in plain sight.

"You're taking one hell of a chance," Ardmore said.

Frank's nerves must have been close to breaking because he said, "Goddammit, I know that!"

We started scrambling through the talus rocks toward the Navajos, and the spokesman yelled out to Begay.

"He say, other *belecana* come too or they kill us all."

I started to sweat. Who knew what Buck would do?

But I guess he figured that alone he'd never get away from the Navvies. I could hear him swear as he came along behind us.

The Navajos began appearing in front of us.

One of them was an old man with a million wrinkles in his sun-blackened face. But he stood aloof and waiting, and anybody could tell he was the leader.

"That Hoskinini, I think," Begay said.

The old Indian looked at Begay and motioned him to come close, then spoke long and sharply to him.

Begay gave him a soft, respectful reply, then turned to us. "He Hoskinini, like I think. He say, what you do in his country? He don't let no *belecanas* here. This not part of reservation. It belong him and his people."

"What did you tell him?"

"I say I ask you."

"It *is* part of the reservation," Frank said. "Since 1890, I think. Tell him we look for the half-*belecana* that killed a judge."

Begay relayed the words and listened to the chief's reply.

"He say the half-*belecana* is Dinéh on his mother's side. That make him Navajo."

"Ask him where Tolbert is now."

The chief must have understood the question, at least in part. He shook his head.

"Does he speak English?" I said.

The chief nodded and spoke to Begay again in Navajo.

"He remember some," Begay said. "He remember from time when the *belecanas* take him to jail for year. He say he don't ever forget that. He say he don't give Tolbert up."

Lola suddenly spoke. "Tell him that if harm comes to us, the *belecanas* will send soldiers to take him to jail again."

Begay said, "I don't like tell him that."

"Tell him!" It was a command.

Reluctantly, he turned to the chief who had a frown on his face, probably because he'd understood.

Begay repeated her words, and that reminded me that Navajos take advice from their womenfolks, unlike a lot of other Indians.

Not that Lola was one of *his* womenfolks, even if she did act like one sometimes, lately.

The old chief thought about what she'd said, then he spoke directly to her. "You leave now, be no trouble."

"Others will come," Lola said. "This time, it wasn't just a prospector killed. This time it was an important judge."

Hoskinini seemed not to have understood all of that, and Begay interpreted.

I thought maybe that would get a sharp rise out of the old chief, but it didn't. Instead, he spent a long time pondering over it.

The other Navajos just stood around, staring at us. It was plain that Hoskinini was the man in charge.

Finally, he turned to a couple of his men and gave an order. The two disappeared into the heavy talus behind them.

"What's going on?" Frank said.

The chief grunted something, and Begay said, "He say wait."

Ardmore said sourly, "I guess we're not going anyplace. We should have taken our chances in a fight."

The two Navvies came back, and they had an unarmed man between them.

"Tolbert!" Frank said.

Tolbert gave him a long, searching look. "Who are you?"

"Frank Ladd, dammit, Ike!" Frank sounded a little put out. "Don't you recognize me?"

"You changed some."

Frank scowled. "So have you."

Hoskinini cut in with a short comment. Tolbert looked puzzled, and Begay said something and Tolbert nodded and said, "I thought that's what he said."

It was kind of plain that he'd forgot a lot of the Navvy lingo.

He was moderately tall, and still lean. He'd been a good-looking breed at one time, I'd guess, but his face now showed the years of suffering. If it wasn't that he'd killed the judge the way he did, I'd have felt sorry for him.

He spoke to Frank. "The chief said I should speak to you. I will say this, Ladd—Why don't you leave me alone?"

Frank said, "There's five thousand dollars on your head, Ike."

"I did my time. I paid the price."

Frank nodded. "Then you spoiled it all, in the matter of the judge."

"He had it coming. Five years would have been enough."

"You can't kill a man because you hate him," Ladd said. "Not even in Arizona anymore. We're in the twentieth century, Ike."

Tolbert gave him a long, studying look. He said finally, "You like that, Frank?"

"No," Ladd said. "I liked the old days better. But that's

how it is. There's been a lot of changes while you were locked up."

"Must have been."

"If I don't bring you in, somebody else will, sooner or later."

"Later would be better. I got twenty years of living to make up." He paused. "I won't be taken alive, Frank. You ready for that?"

"If I have to be. I was hoping it wouldn't be that way."

"I won't be locked up again. Anyway, after a while, they'd hang me. A bullet would be better."

"Your choice," Ladd said.

"Five thousand dollars on my head," Ike said. "Would you do it if it was only one?"

"Maybe not. I always felt you got a raw deal. The money makes the difference."

Tolbert's glance took in Lola. "You got a woman in your posse? That a twentieth century change?"

"My wife," Ladd said.

"Things *have* changed!" Tolbert had a look of wonderment on his face, then it passed.

Ladd said, "Did you think you could hide out up here forever? That these people would protect you?"

"I hoped. They've helped me some."

"It appears there's a limit to their help, maybe."

Tolbert was silent for a spell. Then he said, "The railroads still as powerful as they was?"

"More so," Ladd said. "And growing every day."

"Sorry to hear that."

"You still got thoughts of getting even?"

"Been thinking on it for twenty years."

"Nowadays you wouldn't stand a chance," Ladd said. "They got guards, detectives, electric signal systems you couldn't savvy, and engines as big as a ship."

"I seen one since I been out. It was stopped at Flagstaff when I come through."

"What did you think?"

"Same thing I always thought. I hate the sonsofbitches."

Hoskinini suddenly interrupted, his old lined face drawn into a scowl. His words sounded as fierce as he looked.

Begay said, "He say, what all the talk about? He want to know if you *belecanas* let Tolbert alone."

Hoskinini's eyes were on Frank. Frank shook his head.

There was a short period then when nobody said a word. Then Frank said, "Ike, let me take you in alive. You couldn't stay here for long anyway. Word would get out where you are, and there'd be no end to bounty hunters coming in. I just got the jump on the others."

"Except for me," Buck Ardmore reminded him. "I'm in for half, now."

Ladd ignored the comment, but Tolbert seized on it.

"Half? You got to split the five thousand, Frank? You'd put me behind bars again for half of that?"

"I don't figure on splitting it," Ladd said.

"I don't understand."

"You don't need to. That's my problem."

I was thinking then that it could be a big problem. But there were more urgent matters to contend with right now.

Such as old Chief Hoskinini.

It was plain to see that he was getting impatient with all the *belecana* lingo that was going on. He understood some probably, but not all, and that was making him suspicious.

I hated to see that happen, what with a dozen armed Navvies standing by after a truce they likely hadn't wanted in the first place. It had to've been the old chief's idea to accept it, although he may have been near as reluctant as they were.

Lola spoke up again, to Begay. "Remind him again that if he gives refuge to Tolbert they'll send in soldiers to take him to jail."

"Better you tell him," Begay said.

"All right, I will." She faced Hoskinini and spoke out in firm, slow English.

This time he appeared to understand it all. Once again his ancient face drew into a thoughtful frown. He turned then to Tolbert and spoke in slow Navajo.

Tolbert's body sagged. He said nothing.

Begay did not translate until Lola said to him, "Well?"

"He tell Tolbert he don't can stay here. Too much risk for the Dinéh."

"And?"

Begay hesitated, then went on, sounding nearly as disappointed as Tolbert looked. "He say he give Tolbert chance to get away. He keep us from follow three days."

"He'll hold us while Tolbert runs?"

"That so, he say."

We were all listening, of course.

"Wherever will he go?" Lola said.

Frank said, "Wherever it is, it'll be off the reservation." He motioned us then to withdraw slightly for a discussion. Nobody interfered. "We may lose him for good." He spoke in a low voice so that Tolbert couldn't hear. "In three days he could be deep in Utah, or even in Colorado."

Ardmore said, "We never should have given up our guns, goddammit!"

Frank gave him a disgusted look.

I said, "Begay can pick up his trail. Three days won't wipe it out, barring rain. And rain isn't likely this time of year."

"Don't reckon we've got any choice," Frank said. "Not if the old chief's mind is made up." He kept staring at Tolbert, studying his face. Then he walked close to him again and said, "Ike, you don't stand a chance of going far. Best give yourself up to me."

"Would you do it, if you was in my place?" Tolbert said.

Frank was honest enough not to answer that. Of course he wouldn't. Hell, Tolbert had nothing to lose by running.

Hoskinini spoke again to Begay, and Begay said to us, "He say, you understand?"

"Three days?"

"That what he say, Hosteen."

"Like I said, I don't guess we got a choice."

Begay nodded. "I think so, Hosteen. No choice. No choice for Tolbert, too."

"So be it," Frank said. He nodded to Hoskinini.

The chief gave some rapid-fire orders in Navajo, and his men went into action. Some of them walked to where we'd dropped our weapons, and on to where we'd tethered our horses.

The others gestured with their guns for us to come along and walked to where their own mounts were hidden. Tolbert went with the chief, talking to him, gesturing in a restrained way, as the Navvies always seemed to do.

But all the chief did was shake his head, and when we reached the animals he got stiffly into his saddle. It struck me then that he was getting close to the end of his years. His word, though, was plainly the law to these Navvy dissidents of the north.

When we were all together, we rode toward a larger butte a few miles to the northeast. It was big enough to be called a small mesa.

The odd thing was that Hoskinini, for some reason of his own, motioned Ladd to ride beside Tolbert. The chief rode on the opposite side of Ike, and these three were in the lead.

I kept eyeing them, wondering if there was some strange satisfaction the old chief got out of placing them together. After a few minutes I eased my way up close enough to overhear anything they might have to say to each other.

Begay, for reasons of his own, did likewise. Nobody tried to stop us.

After a while I heard Tolbert speak to Frank. "You got to hunt men for bounty again, Frank? I heard you was famous."

"The years pass," Frank said. "Things change, Ike."

"I reckon. But the years pass a hell of a lot slower in prison. You any idea how that is?"

"Some, maybe. But not really, I guess. A man would have to do time to really know."

"That's for damn sure! Had I knew what I was in for, I'd have let you die of thirst down there in the Pinacate that time."

"You'd have died, too."

"Maybe. But it would've been better than what I went through afterward," Ike said.

"I reckon I can understand that."

"So, you must know now that you'll have to kill me to take me. You up to that, Frank, remembering it was me that led you to water that time?"

"You had to drink too."

"You were nearer to dying than I was. My Injun blood gave me an edge there, and you know it."

Frank was silent.

Tolbert went on, "You owe me something for that. Didn't it ever bother you, over the years?"

"Reckon it did some," Ladd said.

"Well, then."

"Well, then, what?"

"Get off my trail. It'd be a way to pay me back."

"Maybe I could if you hadn't killed that judge the way you did."

"What the hell do you care about him? He was no friend of yours."

"Ain't what I meant. If you hadn't cut off his head and stuck it on a picket post, so as to shock the whole state, there wouldn't be five thousand dollars bounty on you."

"Money that important to you?"

"What else? Why did you rob the trains in the old days, if it wasn't for the money?"

Tolbert said, "It wasn't the money I did it for. I did it to get back at the goddamned railroads. For what they done to me."

"And now? You still feeling revengeful toward them?"

"You goddamned right I am!" Tolbert said, loud and bitter.

After that, he shut up, as if he figured it was doing no good to try to get Frank off his trail.

It went the way Hoskinini said it would. He kept us under guard on the east side of that butte-mesa close to a scattering of hogans that must have been a kind of headquarters for him.

We had a long three days, with nothing to do but lie around under the watchful eyes of the armed Navvies, and the wide, curious eyes of some little kids. The women brought us meals of mutton and fried bread, and they seemed as curious almost as the kids. I'd have bet a lot of them had never even seen whites before, the way they stared.

It was hard to believe they could stay so isolated in the year 1915. The kids were bright little buttons, though, and I think Lola fell in love with most of them.

Tolbert left shortly after we arrived there. He was taking advantage of all the headstart the old chief was giving him.

I think Hoskinini didn't like what he figured he had to do, and he avoided us completely during the wait.

Toward the end Ardmore got increasingly restless. He said, "It'll be damned hard to pick up a cold trail."

"Begay can do it," Frank said.

"Listen, that sonofabitching Indian tried to bushwack me on the mountain. You expect me to ride along with *him*?"

"Not at all," Frank said. "You ain't one of our party, and I don't want you along at all."

"That's gratitude!" Buck said. "You'd be dead now if I hadn't sided you when these red bastards attacked you."

That got to Frank a little. What Buck said was probably true. "Why did you, Buck?"

Ardmore couldn't quite hide a grin. "Hell, you know why. You're the one who'll lead me to that half-breed judge-killer. In fact, you already have. Now, at least, I know what he looks like."

"I can't keep you from following," Frank said. "But, by God! I'll not have you in our camp."

Ardmore's grin widened. "How're you going to stop me?"

"You said you wouldn't ride with Begay, and he's our tracker. When we leave, he rides armed. That hand is healing. He may kill you while you sleep."

"I'll kill the sonofabitch first," Ardmore said.

"You do and we'll lose Tolbert completely. How good a tracker are you, Buck? You done all your law duty inside a town."

"All right, that part," Ardmore said, grudgingly. "But I got to eat. I already ate what grub I carried in my saddlebags. You wouldn't let a white man starve, would you, Frank?"

"I sure as hell would," I said.

"I wasn't asking you."

"His answer is my answer," Frank said.

"You forgetting I saved your skin, Frank?"

Frank was slow to answer. Then he said, "We're running low ourselves. But I'll give you enough to subsist till you get off the reservation. You're on your own then."

"Where do you think he went, Frank? Tolbert, I mean."

"New Mexico, maybe. Maybe Utah. Even Colorado. Lot of places he could hide, if we lose his trail."

"All right, I won't shoot this sonofabitching Indian unless he takes up his grudge."

Begay listened to all this, showed no emotion, and made no comment. I could see he was making Buck nervous, and I figured that was what he wanted to do.

"By God!" Buck said, after staring at Begay and not reading him at all, "I think I *will* make my own camp. That red bastard gives me the willies."

"Good!" Frank said.

Just then a couple of Navajo squaws brought us two big bowls of mutton stew and fried bread. I began to wonder if that was all they ever ate, or if it was all we got because we were prisoners. They were blank-faced when they brought the food, showing neither enmity or friendliness.

The food wasn't bad-tasting, but I found it hard to stomach dipping it with our fingers out of community bowls the way the Navvies do. I managed to get beside Lola, thinking to share with her, but then Begay moved in too and spoiled it all for me.

I almost had to laugh though when I looked over and saw Ladd having to share with Ardmore. Neither one of them liked that at all.

Finally, the three days were up, and the old chief was as good as his word. He came to us for the first time since he'd taken us captive, and said something to Begay.

"He say we go now," Begay said.

"What about our guns?" Frank said.

But a couple of the Navajos were already bringing them, and some others came leading our saddled mounts and the pack animal.

Hoskinini stared coldly at us and went into a short harangue in Navvy. He stopped then and turned away and went back to one of the hogans and disappeared inside.

The other Navajos stood around and watched as we mounted up to leave. None of them spoke.

I asked Begay, "What was that he said at the last?"

"He say go now, and don't never come back. He say too, he wish us much bad luck."

Well, you couldn't blame him for that.

CHAPTER 14

WE set off fast on Tolbert's trail, Begay tracking. It wasn't hard to pick out his sign, and Frank was mostly concerned that Ike had just too much lead and that once he got off the reservation there were a lot of places he could disappear to.

I think he was maybe thinking of Utah, just across the San Juan River, wild country where Butch Cassidy and his kind had frequently hid out.

Every time Begay slowed to study the trail Frank got more and more impatient. "Dammit! Begay, keep moving. He's got three days' lead!"

It seemed, even to me, that Begay's pace was getting slower than it should be.

Buck Ardmore spoke up then. "He's dogging it, Frank. You so blind you can't see that? One goddam Indian helping a half-breed."

Frank scowled. Maybe he was giving it some thought.

Buck said, "Let me take the lead. I can read trail sign faster than he's doing."

Begay overheard him, and dropped back. His jaw had a stubborn set. "Let him, Hosteen," he said.

Maybe Frank decided a change was what we needed if we were ever going to catch up. Maybe he was just on edge from Begay's cautious pace. Or maybe he just thought he'd put that obnoxious Ardmore to the test and see if he'd fall on his face.

Whatever it was, he said, "Go ahead. Move up front, if you think you can cut it."

Well, Buck had us going at a fast walk in no time. He kept it up most of that first day. We made another dry camp, come nightfall. Buck ate with us, but he laid his bedroll a short distance away. None of us thought we needed a guard posted.

The dawn rolled around without mishap. Except for one thing. When we awoke, Buck Ardmore was gone, and he'd taken our pack mule and all our supplies.

Begay was first up and first to notice. I heard him awakening Frank and it awoke me—fast, as I caught his words.

"Hosteen!" he was saying, "That sumbitch white-eyes, he steal mule!"

Frank came out of his blankets as fast as I did.

"Where? When, goddammit?"

Begay shook his head.

"Didn't you hear him?"

Begay shook his head again. "I wake up, he be gone."

"I knew I shouldn't trust that bastard. We should have taken turns at guard," Frank said.

"Too late to worry about that now," I said. "He figured he could track Tolbert all right, and decided to go it alone."

"He couldn't track in the dark."

"Hell, it's a half-hour past dawn," I said. "He'd be that much ahead."

Begay left us and moved off, studying the ground. He walked toward where Buck had spread his blankets the night before. We both started after him, but he turned and came back.

"Okay," he said. "He follow Tolbert. We follow him."

"We need that mule," I said.

"He don't get away."

"I hope not. We'll get damned hungry and thirsty if he does."

There were several buttes ahead, and any one of them could be shielding Ardmore from our sight. He'd had time to have at least reached the nearest of them.

Begay seemed to be heading directly for it.

Partway there we came across a broad band of hoofprints

that indicated the recent passing of a flock of sheep. Ardmore's horse and mule tracks could be seen, if you looked close, although sheep can tear up the soil pretty badly. The sheep had gone by a couple days past, by the looks of it.

It was surprising that we never seemed to see any Navajo herders, or even their sheep, although there was sign here and there all over the reservation of their presence. It was sparse grazing, though, and they had to move great distances, and we just never met up with them.

It was on account of the confusion of prints that it was a short while before either Frank or I got suspicious of where Begay was leading us.

Frank caught it first. "Hold up!" he called.

Begay, who was several yards ahead, seemed reluctant. "He go this way, Hosteen!"

"Hell, I know that!" Frank said, pulling up beside him.

Begay waited.

Frank said, "Buck went this way, but I don't see no sign that Ike did."

Begay just looked at us, then down at the trail, not saying anything.

"Well?" Frank said to him.

"You want catch sumbitch white-eyes?" Begay said.

"I also want to catch Tolbert. Why didn't you say something back there? We must have lost Ike's trail at that sheep passing."

"I guess I forget."

"I guess you didn't," I said. All along I'd been getting a strange feeling that Begay's sense of loyalty to his people was making him more and more reluctant to help track Tolbert down. Thinking back, it seemed the turning point might have been when he met Tolbert face to face in Hoskinini's presence. Begay had seemed to like the half-breed, or at least sympathize with him, *chindi* or not.

I said, "You didn't speak because you knew it would give Ike an even bigger lead. Ardmore was right about you."

He didn't deny it.

Still, I couldn't get mad over the way he felt. Instead, I kind of admired him for it.

"So Buck lost the trail," Frank said. "I ought to've known that. Should have been watching closer myself." He seemed to be considering which way to go now that the trail was split: forget the mule and supplies and Ardmore, or keep after him and allow Tolbert to build more lead.

Finally, he said, "How far ahead is he? Ardmore, I mean."

"Maybe around next butte, Hosteen. Maybe he lost, I think."

"If he's lost, he'll slow down," Frank said. "And we got to get them supplies, I reckon. Let's go!" He paused, then said, "By God! Begay, you let me know what's going on, you understand?"

"Sure, Hosteen." Begay led off again, pushing fast.

Lola said, loud enough for Frank and me both to hear, although Begay couldn't, "He's a good man."

"Who?" Frank said.

"Begay."

"Maybe. I ain't so sure."

"He's all we've got," I said.

"Yeah. But once we're off the reservation, it'll be different. We won't need him then." He sounded kind of irritated by the way Lola had come to Begay's defense.

All these buttes we'd been seeing the last few days were beginning to look alike to me. I mean, at first they were fascinating to look at, but after the novelty wore off you began to lose interest.

The one we were approaching soon aroused it again, though.

The arousal came when Begay said, "He in there, Hosteen, maybe. If he know we here, he maybe hide."

"What'll we do?" I said.

Frank was silent, thinking.

Begay patted the carbine fastened to his saddle. "I go

bring him out." He was now wearing only a small bandage Lola had wrapped over the end of his finger stump.

"Without a trigger finger?" I said.

He held up his hand with his middle finger extended. I threw a quick look at Lola because I'd seen the same gesture used with rude meaning by an occasional cowhand. She appeared to be unaware. Begay was simply showing he had another finger he could fire a weapon with. Awkwardly, maybe, but he could do it.

"Wait a minute!" Frank said.

But Begay kicked his mount and disappeared into some heavy brush beyond.

Frank swore, then followed, but slowly. He said nothing to us as we brought up the rear. We could hear the hoofbeats of Begay's horse as he galloped toward the butte.

"The fool!" Lola said.

"He's got a score to settle with Buck," I said.

"But with that wounded hand! And it's my fault."

"He doesn't blame you for it. He blames Ardmore. And he hates him for killing those Navvies. He's been waiting for revenge."

"A poor chance," she said sadly.

"Who knows?" I said.

We approached the butte cautiously.

"I wish he hadn't gone in there," Lola said.

We heard a first burst of rifle-fire just as Frank halted us in the fringe of juniper and greasewood at the edge of a high, sharply sloped talus.

Begay's horse was just ahead of us in the brush, reins trailing. Even as I looked it took a bullet that felled it.

We could see Begay then. He had reached the talus and taken refuge among the big chunks of fallen sandstone. He was partly hid from us, but was peering upward.

I scanned the reddish cliff face, wondering what he was seeing. I saw it then, a faint puff of smoke followed by the sound of a shot, that came from an eroded recess partway up the face.

The recess was carved from a stratum of white volcanic tuff. We had seen other buttes like this on the reservation, and I knew from reading that in prehistoric times there had been great volcanic actions in much of the Southwest. The tuff was unusually porous, a soft rock formed from pressured ash once thrown out from exploding cauldrons.

You could see by the recess how it had eroded far easier than the sandstone it supported. And as the support lessened over the centuries, the heavier chunks of sandstone fell.

This could account for the higher reach of the talus in which Begay was taking cover. And Ardmore, for reasons of his own, had simply climbed the talus to reach the recess as a vantage point in his duel with Begay.

"What did he climb up there for?" I said.

"The sonofabitch is a coward as well as a killer," Frank said. "He thought it'd give him an edge."

"I guess it will."

"Probably so," Frank said.

We could see Ardmore's horse and our mule a little way along the talus. The animals had run some after he left them to begin his climb, no doubt frightened by the first shots. But now they waited. Then, suddenly, the horse spooked and ran off.

"I'd better go get the mule," I said.

"Don't show yourself out there," Frank said.

"Hell, he wouldn't attack one of us!"

"How do you know that?"

"It'd be murder, for cripe's sake!"

"So was killing those Navvies in that canyon."

"But he's a lawman," I said. "At least he was."

"Yeah," Frank said. "But killing comes easy to him. It's just something he used to keep hid."

"We ought to help Begay," Lola said.

I looked at her and she was reaching for her rifle.

"Don't do it, Lola!"

"I'm on Begay's side in this," she said.

"That ain't the point!" Frank said. "You shoot the ex-marshal of Staffold, a white man at that, you'll end up hanging."

She took her hand off her weapon.

"And that goes for all of us," Frank said.

I knew Lola's feeling was partly because she'd shot off Begay's finger, and that put him at a disadvantage.

There was something else, though, that kept coming to my mind. As long as Ardmore was alive, he'd be after a share, if not all, of the reward on Tolbert.

I kept trying to shove that thought away as something she'd not think of, but I knew deep down that wasn't true. She had her eye on that money in a big way. A hell of a lot more so than Frank even.

Studying the positions now of the two men trying to kill each other, I had to wonder a little how they got into that particular situation.

The way I figured it, Buck had climbed a ways up the talus to check on possible pursuit. He might have been surprised to see Begay coming on fast, and had maybe chanced a shot and missed. He edged up for a better position and suddenly found himself battling it out among the fallen chunks of the talus. Maneuvering during the firefight had led him to the recess.

There was another exchange of shots now, then no sight of either of them for a spell, until the sun glinted on a rifle barrel thrust over the recess edge. It belched. Down below, still in some kind of cover, Begay fired back.

Again, we couldn't tell what happened.

"Begay'll get himself killed for sure if he tries to flush Buck out of that hole," Frank said.

"If he stays where he is he'll get killed, too," I said.

"Let me help him, Frank," Lola said.

"No, goddammit!" Frank said. "I told you why." He

paused. "We're losing time. We ought to ride on and leave these two damn fools to have at it."

"No," Lola said. "We've got to stay. There may be some other way we can help Begay."

"Dammit, Lola! Have you fell in love with that Injun?"

"I owe him to stay," she said. "For what I did to him."

I said, "He seems to shoot all right with his spare finger."

"You don't know that," she said. "I know better. A thing like that can make a world of difference. We've got to wait, Frank."

"All right," Frank said. "For a short while. But that's all. If this ain't over quick, we're moving on. I'm guessing Tolbert lit out for the San Juan River crossing at Mexican Hat, and that's where we're going."

She didn't say anything more to that.

Begay suddenly fired again, a series of shots. I looked to see what he was aiming at, because at the moment there was no sight of Ardmore, except that his weapon again appeared.

I couldn't see where Begay's bullets were hitting. I'd have expected to see puffs of debris flying from around the extended barrel of Ardmore's rifle, but this wasn't so.

Buck continued to shoot down into the talus, but he must not have had a fix on Begay, because Begay was still spacing out his own shots, even though I couldn't see his target.

Something caused me to raise my eyes then to the slanting ceiling above the recess. It was greatly eroded by storm seepage through cracks in the loosened sandstone, and by centuries of blasting wind.

As I watched, I could see spurts of loosened stone flying out from around an immense, lowering chunk of sandstone. It must have weighed half a ton.

The hanging chunk was directly above where Buck had concealed himself.

"By God!" I said. "I don't think Buck knows what Begay is up to. Not yet, anyway!"

"What is it?" Lola said.

"Up there, above his head."

She and Frank must have seen what I saw then. For a moment we were all struck dumb by the sight.

Then Frank said, "If Begay has enough shots. . . ."

"Or if Buck doesn't look up," I said.

Lola said, "Oh, God! Begay, do it! Do it!"

She cried out again then, as Begay rose slightly to get a better aim at the loosening slab and Ardmore's bullet struck him. Begay threw up his hands, dropping the Winchester, and fell backwards over the talus rocks.

I caught that out of the corner of my eye. Because my stare was on the huge chunk of sandstone as it fell.

I knew it was going to crush Ardmore, even as his rifle jerked backward, then flew up again out of his grasp.

When we reached Begay's body, we saw the bullet hole that had drilled his head.

Lola began to cry. She said, "We've got to bury him!"

"We will," Frank said.

He and I began climbing upward, leaving her there.

When we reached Buck, we were both sick at what we saw. He was smashed to where he was unrecognizable. I couldn't speak. What the hell could I say?

Frank said it. "Well, Begay got his revenge for those kinfolks Buck slaughtered."

CHAPTER 15

NOW Frank was totally concerned with getting back on Tolbert's trail.

He had been depending heavily on Begay, and although at one time he must have been a fair tracker, a lot of years had gone by since then. Then there was the matter of his eyes. He wasn't as sharp with them as he might once have been—in more ways than one.

Lola and I were both aware of this. We got so that while Frank was concentrating on trying to read trail sign, we'd ease our boredom by playing games. Flirting, I guess was the real word for it. Looking at each other, making eye contact, exchanging guarded smiles. Sex signals, or at least they were on my part. And if I was reading her right, on her part too.

And Frank didn't seem to notice any of this. At least not at first. We got so we were pretty open about it. Maybe it lent a little more excitement that way, added a little more spice to the game.

Frank's only comments during this time referred to Tolbert.

"Ike's got a hell of a lead, if he takes advantage of it," he said a couple of times. Or, "A trail this cold is damned hard to follow." Once he said, "Maybe I can just outguess him. I always was good at reading people and figuring out what was going on in their minds."

I almost laughed in his face when he said that. I glanced at Lola and there was a wicked little smile tugging at her lips and she winked at me.

As usual, Frank didn't notice that either.

He cut northward slightly and picked up the trail he

thought led to Mexican Hat. "It's my guess that's where Ike struck out for," he said. "There's a bridge there, I understand. One of the few places you can get across the San Juan."

So we rode fast, hoping he was right.

"You ever been there, Frank?" I said.

He shook his head. He had out his map. "It can't be much further, according to this. Maybe we'll hit it before nightfall."

But we didn't, and so we made camp at dusk.

Later, when it came time to turn in, Frank said suddenly, "Drew, you and me will take turns standing watch tonight. I been thinking, since Ardmore run off with our mule the way he did, some Navvy might just do the same. Until we get out of their country at least."

His words made sense to me. It was going to cut hell out of our sleeping time, though.

"You can take the first stint, Drew. From now till midnight. And I'll take it from then to first light."

"No," Lola said. "I'll do my share. You two need more sleep than that."

"All right," Frank said. "You take it from now to eleven, say. You wake Drew then and he can take it till two. I'll take it from there."

He reached in his pocket and took out his watch and gave it to her. "I got the only timepiece, so we'll pass it along." He paused. "Fair enough, Drew?"

"Fair enough," I said. We had our blankets spread out in a kind of depression to get some protection in case the wind sprang up as it did sometimes at night. "But we can't see much out of this hollow."

"You're right," Frank said. "Lola, go up on that knoll there. That'll be the place to see from. And take your bedroll. It could get cold later on."

She picked up her blankets and made her way up there. It was maybe fifty yards away.

"We'd best turn in, Drew," he said to me. "Get all the sleep you can."

I crawled into my blankets, but I couldn't get to sleep for a long time. Frank began to snore almost at once, but that wasn't what kept me awake.

What did was thinking about Lola lying up there alone, and me wishing I was with her.

I dozed off finally. It must have been about ten when I awoke, judging by the stars. The dream I was having about her was what woke me, and I woke up breathing hard.

I got up quick. It was as if I couldn't help myself. I glanced over at Frank's dark form, lying unmoving. He was snoring still.

The next thing I knew I was up there on the knoll, and I was looking down at her figure stretched out on her blanket. There was no wind and the air had stayed warm, and she had no cover over her. At first I thought she'd fallen asleep, but then she spoke in a whisper.

"I thought you'd never come," she said.

"I had to think it over," I said.

"What's to think?"

"About Frank."

"He sleeps sound when he sleeps."

"Not what I meant."

"What did you mean?"

"Taking what belongs to him," I said.

"Oh, Drew. You're such a young fool."

"Why?"

She hesitated then, and when her whisper came again it was harsh with resentment. "Don't you know? He hasn't been able to take what belongs to him for years!"

It took a few seconds for me to get what she meant..

"Drew," she said, "get down here before I kill you!"

I did.

And then, almost at once, I heard his boots stomping up the slope, and I began to fight her loose. I couldn't get her arms from around my neck. She had her mouth pressed hard against mine and I couldn't tell her what I heard.

I panicked.

I guess it finally got through to her what I was trying to do, and she let go of me. She pushed away like she was mad.

I stood up so Frank could see me. I pretended to be sweeping the dark landscape with my eyes, timing it so that I swung to face his approach while he was still a few yards away.

"Changing guard, Drew?" he said.

I didn't answer at once. I was trying to decide if he was sincere or sarcastic. My fingers reached down to touch my revolver. I remembered then that I'd left it lying by my bedroll, along with my carbine.

I saw him raise a weapon.

Lola was sitting up, and I heard her gasp.

"Listen, Frank . . . " I started to say.

"I brought your carbine up," he said. "When you stand guard, you'd best have something to shoot with." He handed it to me. "Is it eleven o'clock already, Lola?"

"Close," she said. "Very close."

"Best give my watch to Drew, then," he said. "So he'll know when to wake me up." He paused. "Lucky I woke when I did, Drew, and saw you'd forgot your gun."

I didn't say anything. I still wasn't sure if he was leading me on.

"Come on, Lola," he said. "Time you turned in and got some sleep."

"Yes, Frank," she said, and went with him as he started down off the knoll.

She left her blankets for me, and that's all I got from her that night.

I also got an hour more of guard duty than I should have had.

And one of the worst scares of my life.

The next morning there were no more games between us.

I didn't want to do anything that might get Frank to thinking about what happened last night. If he started giving thought to it, he might see there was more there than he suspected.

I guess Lola felt the same way. The few times our eyes met, she turned away quick. I hoped she hadn't scared as badly as I had. I knew I'd get over my fright, because I was driven by desire. I wasn't that sure about her.

I consoled myself with thinking how aggressive she'd been there on her blanket. I was pretty certain then that there'd be another opportunity before long. Dammit! There had to be.

Just about then Frank suddenly said, "About last night, Drew . . . "

A chill took me.

" . . . Any time you're standing watch, you want to be armed. I'd think you'd know that, boy."

"I won't make that mistake again," I said, and I meant it.

"You're learning, Drew. You're learning," he said. "I've got a lot of confidence in you. This is all a new experience for you."

I would agree with that, all right.

"Do you think Ike will head into Utah?" I said.

"Could well be. Once we reach Mexican Hat, I'll inquire around. We might turn up a lead. If not, I'll play my hunches. That worked out well for me many a time in the old days. Sometimes you have to work on a sixth sense, more than what are the known facts." He paused. "Especially if there ain't none."

That didn't make much sense to me, but I had to figure he knew what he was talking about, even if I didn't.

"Should be easy going till we reach there," he said. "It can't be far ahead." It was farther than he thought, though. It was late afternoon when we got there.

Mexican Hat lay in a desert valley just north of the San Juan River, and we crossed on a suspension bridge to reach it. Actually the town was called Goodridge, after a prospector and oil exploration official who founded it. But a lot of folks called it Mexican Hat because there was a rock formation nearby that looked like a big sombrero.

There were also some deserted-looking oil derricks around it.

There was a store and some other buildings there, and we stopped at the store to buy some provisions we needed. We pumped the storekeeper a little for information, but we didn't find out much because he was mostly interested in booming the town to us.

Mr. E.L. Goodridge, he told us, had found the first indications of oil a few years back while he was prospecting for gold. He'd managed to get the financial backing to drill a well, and he brought in a gusher.

"They say it shot sixty feet into the air," the storekeeper said proudly. "That's when they finally built the bridge."

"The place doesn't look like a boomtown," I said.

He gave me a half-angry look, then relented. "It was for a while," he said. "There were more than twenty drilling rigs here at one time."

"What happened?"

"Most of the holes were dry," he said reluctantly. "A little oil and gas out of a few, but nothing worthwhile commercially. Wasn't any more gushers, that's for sure. And things quieted down some then."

"It appears so," Frank said.

"It's still a nice little town," the merchant said.

"It seems to be," Lola said. "I noticed there's a hotel. Could a lady get a bath there?"

"She most certainly could, ma'am. And overnight accommodations. That's if they've got a room vacant."

Frank said gruffly, "Me and Drew don't need accommodations. You got any whisky on sale here?"

"Try the saloon. I gave up handling booze when there was all those roustabouts around. The money I made on it wasn't worth the trouble they caused me."

He laid out the foodstuffs we'd asked for. "You folks traveling to see the scenery?"

"More or less," Frank said. "A friend of ours was to meet us here. Going to guide for us, really. Fella had some Injun blood in him. Would be riding a pinto horse, most likely. Maybe you've seen him?"

The storekeeper looked thoughtful. "Nope. Can't say that I have. But then I don't get out on the street much. You might ask around town, though." He paused. "Had Indian blood, you say?"

"Some," I said. "Part Navajo."

"Navajo, huh? Well, he might be a good enough guide up here, but if you're going into the Utah wilds, a Ute would be better."

"This one is a personal acquaintance," Frank said. "You don't think I'd take my wife on a camping trip with some strange Injun, do you?"

"I didn't mean no offense. I kind of forgot about the lady. There's *some* Navajos that know the Utah wilds, I guess. I ain't really an authority on Indians."

"This is one I've known for twenty years," Frank said.

"I reckon you can trust one you've known that long." The storekeeper toted up the bill on a pad of paper and gave Frank the total.

Frank took out what was left of his money and paid him, and shoved the rest back into his pocket. There didn't seem to be much left.

"Thanks, folks," the storekeeper said.

Outside, Lola said, "Frank, I've got my mind set on that hotel room. A single wouldn't cost much."

"We'll see," Frank said. "We'll see."

A thought came to me about then, and I looked at her.

She seemed to feel my eyes on her, and turned to face me.

We kept staring at each other while we walked toward where we'd hitched the horses, and I almost fell off the porch because of it.

I caught myself as I stumbled, and I heard her laugh. I didn't resent the laugh, though, because I knew then she had read what I was thinking.

And if she laughed, she must have been pleased about it.

A lot of possibilities came to my mind.

We stashed the food on the animals, then Frank said, "I'm going to the saloon yonder." He nodded across the street. "I'll have a drink and ask the bartender does he recall a stranger passing through, and suchlike. You coming along with me for a drink, Drew?"

Well, I wanted one, but there was something else I wanted more.

"I'll wait here with Lola," I said. "I don't like to see her waiting here alone."

He gave me an odd look. "Well now, Drew, that's mighty considerate of you." He hesitated. "I won't be long."

I learned something about Frank then that I'd never suspected. He had an occasional urge to get drunk. He got it very rarely, Lola told me later, and only when his frustrations got too great for him to keep the lid on.

This wasn't something entirely out of the normal, I suppose. Many a man has such inclinations from time to time. But Frank's weakness here took me by surprise.

The tip-off was when, a short while later, he came out of the saloon with a quart of whisky in each hand.

I started to comment, but Lola touched my arm and said, "Let him, Drew. For God's sake, let him!" Her fingers tightened in a series of quick, urgent squeezes. She was sending a message, as clear as Morse code to a telegrapher, one that brought a flush to my loins.

"Frank," she said to Ladd, "we've got a little money left, and I want to sleep in a hotel bed for one night while I've still got the chance."

He'd already drunk down a third of one bottle. He offered me a drink that I took, then he poured a long slug down his own throat. He stared at her sort of blankly while the drink was hitting bottom. He took another, choked a little, then said, "Sure, Lola, why not? It's been a long, tough trail for you. You go get yourself a room. Drew and me will make camp just outside town somewheres." He drank again. "Tomorrow, though, we got to try and pick up ol' Ike's trail." He hiccupped. "Ol' Ike," he said.

All that liquor was hitting him hard.

I looked at Lola, thinking she might be getting mad. Instead, there was a faint smile on her face when she exchanged glances with me. A faint smile, and something more. A promise of a lust of her own.

"Drew," Frank said, "soon as we make camp, you roam around and see if you can pick up a word on a half-breed riding a pinto, you hear?"

"I hear, Frank," I said.

"Lola, get yourself that room," he said. "Drew, you and me will find a spot to spread our blankets. Later, you go by that livery stable yonder and leave the animals. They damn sure could use some grain."

"That they could, Frank."

"You damn betcha," he said. He shoved the whisky bottles into a saddlebag, got a boot into the near stirrup and hauled up. He didn't quite clear his right leg over the cantle and his toe kicked the horse in the haunch and it shied.

"Whoa, goddammit!" he said.

My concern now was that he didn't somehow bust those bottles before he emptied them.

Because Lola was walking fast down the street toward the hotel. I was sure hoping there was a vacancy.

He passed out right after dark.

I was afraid to rush things, though. Instead, I waited an hour or so to make sure he wasn't going to wake up. Hell, he didn't even stir, just lay there like he was dead. I finally lit a match over him to make sure he wasn't just lying there with his eyes open. I could see the regular rise and fall of his chest then, and he looked to me like he was going to be sawing logs for the rest of the night.

I left in a hurry then. I couldn't wait any longer. I could still hear the words she'd spoken to me the previous night, before he'd interrupted us. When she'd said, "Drew, get down here with me before I kill you!"

When I had taken the horses to the livery stable I had stopped at the hotel on the way back. She was waiting in the lobby. I'd stayed just long enough to get her room number.

Now, entering the lobby, there was no clerk in sight at the desk in the little alcove. I slipped by and climbed the rickety stairs. There couldn't have been more than six rooms down and six up. She was in number twelve, at the far end of a lamplit hallway.

She must have been waiting for me, because the door opened as soon as I knocked.

"Did he drink himself into a stupor?" she said.

"Yeah. Does it happen often?"

"Never more than once or twice a year. All that booze around him at Morency's place and he never lets it get the best of him. Then, six months, a year, and some night he lets go. It's strictly a one-night thing."

"Well, I'm glad he has that failing. Tonight, I mean."

"I'm glad, too. The first time I've ever been glad that he's drunk."

"Then I'm the first?"

"The first ever, Drew. Though, God knows, I've been tempted."

"I wondered about that," I said. "You being a lot younger than him."

"Drew, I didn't give you my room number so we could talk." She was taking off her blouse as she said it.

"I didn't figure so." My throat was getting dry as I said it.

During the next minute we had a sort of stripping contest.

I got her on the bed, and once I had her in my embrace all I had to do was hold on.

The only kind of woman I'd ever had before, I'd paid for. And although some of them had pretended passion, I always knew it was playacting.

There was no playacting here.

Well, I was equal to it. At least for a while.

But there came a time. And then we just lay there holding hands, and she began to talk.

"It's been a long time, Drew," she said. "When I met Frank, he was approaching middle-age, but he was a hell of a man in bed still. And I was crazy about him." She turned her head on the pillow and gave me a searching look. "I'm telling you this because I want you to understand."

"Understand what?"

"How it was. And how it is."

"How is it, Lola?"

"The same way it always was. Frank's mine, and I'm his."

"And this, then?"

"Can't you understand?"

I was silent, thinking about it. Then I said, "No, Lola, I don't think I can. I want you—for keeps."

"Drew, Drew, you've got so much to learn," she said. She kissed me then, and squeezed my hand, and we just lay there, and pretty soon we fell asleep.

When I awoke I had no way of knowing what time it was, and I jumped out of bed, and that woke her too.

"Going someplace, Drew?" She sounded sleepy and satisfied.

"Hell, yes!" I said. "I better!"

She came fully awake then. "I'd forgot!"

"Me, too. I wonder what time it is."

"I don't know. I hope it's not near morning yet."

"I hope not!" I was getting into my clothes fast. "About

Frank," I said. "What do you think he'd do if he knew about this?"

I couldn't see her clearly in the dark.

"I don't know," she said.

"He could kill me."

"He could."

"You sound damned casual about it."

"I don't know," she said, "because, like I told you, I never did this to him before."

"Christ!" I said. "Frank Ladd!"

"Are you scared?"

"No," I lied.

"You be a brave boy, Drew, and maybe it'll all work out."

That stung me, and I said, "He could damned well kill you too."

By her silence, I knew I'd hit home with that. I worked at getting my boots on.

Then she said, "Come kiss me, Drew."

I went to the bed and leaned over her and put my lips on hers. I could feel my passion rising again, and I could feel her response as her arms tried to tug me down.

I pulled away. "For God's sake, Lola! I've got to get out of here!"

"It may still be early," she said.

"It's more likely late."

"You're right."

I stood up then and went rapidly toward the door. I didn't say anything else.

Just as I stepped out into the hall I heard her crying.

CHAPTER 16

ONCE outside the hotel, I guessed by the sky that there was an hour yet until dawn. And when I arrived at the camp, Frank sounded like he was still sleeping off his drunk. But when morning came, I began to have all sorts of doubts.

His attitude toward me seemed strained. It bothered me to the point that I had to probe, even though I was scared as hell of the answer.

"Frank," I said, "you got something eating on you?"

He gave me a long look without saying anything, and I had the feeling I was in trouble.

"You damned right I have," he said then.

"Well, what is it?" I said. I was trying to think of some lie to give him.

"A hangover," he said.

I was so relieved, I felt cocky. "A man shouldn't overindulge, Frank."

"Yeah," he said. "When a man does that, he's apt to pass out and miss a lot that might be going on."

I lost my cockiness, but I said, "You snored all night long."

He gave me another stare. "And how would you know that?"

"Hell, I laid here and listened to you."

He was still staring. "Is that a fact?"

"What do you mean?"

He just shook his head.

So there I was. We didn't speak again the whole time we were breaking camp.

We went by the hotel to get Lola, and the three of us had coffee there in the little dining room. None of us said much.

We all were wearing poker faces, even Lola. It was like not one of us wanted another to know what we were thinking.

We all tried to avoid looking at one another too, which is hard to do when you're sitting at a little breakfast table.

Finally, Frank said, "Let's go." He went out and led the way to the livery stable. We saddled the horses and packed the mule and rode to the edge of the town.

He pulled a paper out of his pocket then and studied it. It looked like a crude map somebody had drawn for him. I remembered then that neither of us had asked the hosteler for information he might have given about Tolbert. I'd had a bigger worry on my mind.

"He went east out of here," Frank said. "I met a fella in the saloon last night. He said a half-breed-looking bastard on a pinto pony came through a couple of days ago and took the road east toward Cortez."

"Last night? In the saloon?"

His eyes burned into mine now. "I didn't sleep as sound as you might have thought. Woke up after a couple of hours. Went to the bar to ask if anybody'd seen Ike."

I didn't know what to say to that.

"You sleep damn quiet, Drew," he said. "I couldn't hear you at all."

I said the only thing I could think of. "So you think Ike went to Colorado?"

"Went that direction. Asked this fella directions for getting to Cortez. It's near a hundred-mile ride." He paused. "Bartender drew me this map."

I kept trying to concentrate on what he was saying, but it was hard to do. I kept thinking about what he'd said about me sleeping quiet.

"You should have woke me," I said. "I'd have gone with you."

"Never gave it a thought," he said. "Besides, anybody that sleeps that sound must be having pretty pleasant dreams."

I risked a glance at Lola, and she looked as scared as I felt.

"Hundred miles," I said, trying to change the subject. "We'd best be on our way."

"That we had," he said, and led off on the dirt road.

I don't know when I've ever been so ill at ease. There was one thought riding with me during those first few miles: *He suspects!* I fought to get rid of it, and then I wished I hadn't. Because what took its place was: *He knows!*

I guessed that the only reason he didn't make an issue of it right then was that he was too sick from his hangover.

All that it did though, I knew, was give me a brief reprieve.

The reprieve lasted longer than I expected. We rode all morning along a road that ran northeasterly, and in the early afternoon we reached a cluster of brick houses built of the same red adobe-like earth on which they stood. The place was called Bluff. There were some artesian wells there that provided irrigation for some shade and fruit trees.

There was a trading post, too. And a few Navvies around. I guess we were still close to the border of the Navajo country.

Frank said, "Lola, you go in there and see if you can find out any word about our guide."

I hated to be left alone with him, and I said, "I'll go."

"Not you," he said. "Lola will go." And then to her, "When you ask the trader, make it sound sweet. If one of us goes he might think we're hunting somebody down."

"Sweet, Frank?"

"You know what I mean," he said. He gave her a cold stare then. "Use your sex on *him*."

She flushed and bit her lip, then whirled around and stomped into the post.

There were a couple of Navvy bucks standing out front, and they kept staring at us, then looking away when they caught us noticing. They made me even more nervous. I was waiting for Frank to open up on me.

But all the time we waited, he didn't say a word.

In about five minutes Lola came out again. She went right up to Frank and said, "He came through. At least somebody on a pinto did. And took the trail to Cortez, the trader thinks."

I was surprised that she'd got that much information out of him. "How'd you get him to tell you that?"

She looked at Frank coldly. "Sweet talk," she said.

"Sex did it," Frank said. "A woman can get damned near anything she wants if she's good-looking. I figured you knew that by now, Drew."

I said quickly, "We going to camp here?" I was grabbing for something to say.

"We'll push on. Maybe make another fifteen miles before dusk."

And that's what we did.

I spent a restless night. And so did Lola.

I could hear her turning and tossing in her bedroll whenever I was awake, which was often. Frank, though, slept like he was exhausted, or sounded like it. I had the feeling though that he might be lying there awake, too, and just waiting for us to be tempted into something rash.

Believe me, there was no way I was going to be. I'd even made it a point to spread my own blankets several yards away from Lola's, just so he wouldn't get any mistaken ideas.

The next day went pretty much like the previous one. Frank no longer looked hung over, but he was still silent and withdrawn.

For most of the day, the only difference was in the country we rode over. This was mostly a vast plain covered with sage.

I had never seen sage grow so high. In some places it was four or five feet high, and mixed with juniper and piñon. Here and there were canyons cutting through the plain. There was pretty fair grazing too. Good sheep or cattle country, I thought.

But we didn't see any livestock. Maybe because the brush was so high. It was lucky we were following a road of sorts.

Even so, Frank took out the map the Mexican Hat saloonkeeper had drawn for him. He looked at it and started to put it away.

I'd lost some of my scare by now and I was beginning to get irritated. "Mind if I look at that?" I said.

Without a word, he handed it to me.

"Where do you think we are?" I said.

He reached over and stuck his forefinger on a spot that looked a little past halfway between Bluff and Cortez.

"One more day and we'll be there," I said. "I wonder where Ike would go, once he reached it?"

He just shook his head.

I went through another restless night, but not as bad as the last one.

We had just broken camp the next morning when he finally started to open up on me. We were actually in our saddles and I was leading the mule, when he first spoke.

"Drew," he said, "a man gets older and he grows used to putting up with a lot of things he wouldn't have when he was younger."

"I reckon so," I said.

"But there's some things he will not stand for." He'd been staring ahead at the trail, not once looking at me, but now he turned his head and met my eyes full on.

"I will not," he said, "stand for a man trifling with my wife."

I heard Lola gasp.

Well, there it was. And I was damned if I would deny it.

He *knew*, and there was no use trying to lie out of it.

A silence dragged on between us. We were still holding each other's eyes. This was the man who'd always been my hero. Still was, in fact. What had happened between Lola and me didn't change that.

"Don't you have anything to say?" he said. His voice was strained.

"Nothing," I said.

"You goddam cuckolding young bastard," he said. "I ought to blast your balls with my .45."

When I heard the gun go off, I thought for sure that I was dead.

And then I saw it was the pack mule that was down, with blood running out of a hole drilled between its eyes.

The report, a rifle crack really, had come from a distance, not from Frank. It was one big relief when I realized that.

There was behind us a sharply gouged shallow canyon from which we had just climbed. "Take cover!" Frank yelled, and he and Lola raced side by side for it.

I still had the dead mule's lead rope tied to my saddle. I tore at it with my fingers, trying to get it loose.

I heard Frank shout to Lola, "Keep going!" and then he was turning back toward me.

By then I was free, and when he saw that he pivoted again to follow Lola.

But the move he'd made struck me hard. It was a little thing, instinctive maybe. But it told me something about the man. It restored for me the image that recently had begun to tarnish.

But I had no more time to think about it then.

Once down in the cut, we dismounted to peer over the sharp embankment, searching for the point from which the shot had come.

"Had to be dead ahead," he said. "The way it hit the mule."

"He had to be pretty close to get a clear shot through the brush, thick as it is," I said.

"Worst place in the world to have to fight an Injun. He could be anywhere."

"Indian?" I said.

"Half-breed is what I meant."

"Tolbert? How do you know?"

"Just another hunch," he said. "I could be wrong."

"I thought he was days ahead of us yet."

He didn't answer at once. Then he said, "Could be he got tired of running."

"He could have shot you then, instead of the mule."

'He could have," he said. "But he didn't."

"Why?"

"Hell, he was put away for those twenty years, and he sure wasn't allowed to target practice. It's as simple as that. He's rusty."

That made sense. "But he only fired one shot," I said.

"We moved some, even you. Thick as this sage is, he likely couldn't get another bead on us."

Lola was holding the horses, but listening. Now she said, "He's desperate, Frank. He'll kill you if he can. He'll not let himself be locked up again. He told you that."

"I heard him."

"You shoot him if you can. You'll never take him alive anyway. This proves it."

He was staring over the rim of the chasm, as I was, still trying to spot Tolbert, if it was him.

"I can't shoot him if I can't see him," he said.

The full implication of what he said would come back to me later.

I was the one that did the spotting. Tolbert was on a brushy hillock, not two hundred yards away. And all I caught was a glimpse of his Stetson hat and the head and neck of the pinto pony he must have been leading.

"You see him?"

"No. Where?" Frank said.

I looked at him, and his eyes were squinted, even though the sun was behind us. Like he'd once said, his eyes sure weren't too good for distance anymore.

"On that rise, to the left of where the road is headed."

"You think it was Ike?"

"I saw the pinto."

"This is our chance to take him, boy!"

He seemed to have forgotten what he'd been threatening me with a few minutes earlier.

"How?"

"We'll just set tight. He must know we dropped back into this cut. If so, he'll come to us."

"And if he doesn't?"

"If he don't, it means he took to running again. But what would be his reason now?"

"Maybe he doesn't need a reason," I said. "What would be his reason to wait and try to bushwack us? He's acting a little peculiar, seems to me."

"Could be," Frank said. "But I reckon doing prison time for twenty years could addle a man's thinking some."

"Frank, you've got that twenty years on your brain."

"I ain't forgetting it," he said. "Trouble is I also got it on my body." He paused. "Going to take the both of us to catch him, boy."

"Lay it out, then," I said.

"Trouble is, it looks like this damned canyon has got a crook each way in it. One of us will have to take a lookout at that south bend, another to the north there."

"And if he comes straight on?"

"I'll watch from here. It's most likely he'd come this way."

"If I see him, do I shoot him?" I said.

"I reckon that'll be the way it is, Drew."

"I never killed a man before."

"There's a first time for anything," he said.

"Shooting tin cans is one thing, but—"

"I know, boy. But you remember you had a gunfight with him in that bat cave."

"It was him or me, then."

"It'll be him or you now too. Just keep that in mind."

I had it in my mind all right, as I rode south a couple of hundred yards to the bend where I found some rocky cover. When I looked back, I saw he'd sent Lola riding toward the north bend. He'd stayed where he was, there on the east rim.

From my position I could see straight down the cut for a half mile or so. I was hoping that Lola had the same visibility at her end, but there was no way of knowing.

It bothered me that he'd let her get that far away alone. He seemed to have a lot of faith in her ability to protect herself. Another thought struck me then. Maybe he didn't care what happened to either of us.

Somehow, though, I couldn't believe that. It just didn't fit the image of Frank Ladd at all.

We settled down to wait. The sun was hot down in the canyon. And I began to wonder what would happen if Ike crossed the cut somewhere beyond our sight and came at us from the west. Had Frank thought of that?

The longer we waited, the more I worried about it. He'd as much admitted he was getting old for what he was up against, saying it would take all our help to get Ike. It was the first time I'd ever heard him, out and out, admit it.

I was still brooding about this when I heard the revolver blast. I jerked around and could see the smoke up where Frank had been. My first thought was that Ike had got him.

Then I saw him scrambing up over the rim, and he disappeared.

I swung into my saddle and raced up the arroyo bottom. I could see Lola heading back toward me. We arrived at the road almost together, and dismounted and rushed to see where Frank had gone.

Up the trail where the mule lay we could see him standing. Off to one side an excited pinto, reins dropped, was shying around crazily. The thing that shocked me first was that it wasn't Tolbert's pinto.

At Frank's feet was an Indian dressed in Levi's. His high-crowned hat was lying on the ground. He was on his back and blood was welling from a hole in his chest and he wasn't moving.

"Frank," I said, "you've killed the wrong man."

"Ute, by the looks of him."

"How can you tell?"

"Don't see no silver trimmings on him, like the Navvies wear," he said. "Was the reason I thought it was Ike."

"Hell," I said, "that pinto is marked different than Tolbert's. Didn't you notice?"

He had an edge to his voice when he answered. "Drew, when you're face to face in a gunfight, you got no time to check a horse's markings."

"Gunfight?" I said. "He fire that rifle?"

"He had it ready when he got down to check the mule's pack."

"Poor damned Indian," I said. "He should have known we'd be waiting."

"No telling how an Injun thinks," he said. "Which is why I didn't wait to ask him." He paused. "To me he looked like Tolbert."

"Frank, you need your eyes examined."

"I hit him, didn't I?" he said.

A sudden thought made me say, "Were you shooting at his head?"

He looked down at the dead Ute's body, as if to make sure where the blood was flowing from. "I was shooting at his chest," he said.

I said, "The poor bastard came to see what was in the pack he killed the mule for. Hungry, maybe. He figured, or at least hoped, he'd scared us away. Must have been damned hungry or damned dumb."

"I don't feel good about it," he said. "Not one bit."

None of us did. I took the beat-up saddle and bridle from the pinto, and let it run free. We couldn't afford to be caught with it.

We divided up the supplies from the pack, and stashed them here and there on the horses. Then we dragged the dead Ute to the canyon edge and dropped him over a steeper part of the bank. We kicked at the edge until some of it broke loose and fell to cover him.

It wasn't much of a burial, but we couldn't do any more without a shovel. We were mostly interested in hiding him from any other Utes that might come around.

Frank didn't speak a word all the time we were doing this.

Several times I saw him looking at Lola with an expression that seemed to be begging for something. She didn't show him anything in return.

One thing about it, he wasn't now in a mood to berate us for what we'd done. He'd made too bad a mistake himself.

Trading a man's life for a pack mule's didn't strike any of us as a fair exchange.

CHAPTER 17

EARLY the next morning we rode into Cortez, a cattle and sheep town that we found out later from the deputy there was the Montezuma County seat. In spite of that, it had only three or four hundred people.

About the only striking thing there was the several tan sandstone buildings scattered around, mixed with the wood ones.

Frank led us up to the Sheriff's office and jail, which wasn't much bigger than you'd expect, but built of sandstone that made it look hard to break out of. The jail, I mean.

"Wait outside here," he said. "I'll ask."

He didn't have to tell us what he'd ask about. What we had to know was where Tolbert went from here. That is, if he'd ever reached the place. There'd been no way to know, following that used road across the sage country.

Frank was in there quite a while, and we began to get restless.

There was a strained silence between us. It was as if she wanted to tell me something, but couldn't bring herself to it.

I don't think we spoke a word between us all the time we waited.

Fifteen minutes must have passed before Frank came out, and there was a man wearing a star with him. The man looked to be about Frank's age, although he had sort of gone to fat.

They both looked kind of pleased.

"Good news?" I said.

"I want you to meet an old aquaintance of mine," Frank said. "Deputy Sheriff Jake Storm. We go back a long time."

I stepped forward and shook his hand. "Drew Hardin," I said.

His grasp slackened abruptly. "Hardin?" he said.

Frank said, "No relation to John Wesley."

"That's different," Storm said, and his grasp tightened again.

"And my wife, Lola."

Storm doffed his hat, showing a headful of gray hair. "My pleasure, ma'am." He paused. "I recall a few years back it was when I heard Frank had got married."

"Fifteen, to be exact," Lola said.

"Seems like yesterday," the deputy said.

Frank said, "Jake here is acting sheriff. The sheriff died a short while back, and they haven't yet elected anybody. Jake's going to run for it."

"I wish you luck, Mr. Storm," Lola said, and gave him a big smile.

Storm beamed. "Thank you, ma'am."

Frank said, "Jake's big problem is a young sheriff they've got over to Durango in La Plata County," Frank said. "He's great for making headlines, Jake tells me. By comparison, he makes Jake look outdated." Frank slapped Storm on the back. "Just joking, Jake. But I know the feeling."

"I don't take no offense," Storm said. "It's a fact of life that goes with these changing times."

"My sentiments, exactly."

"I liked the old days better," Storm said.

"Who didn't?" Frank said. "But we got to live with the way it is." He turned to me again. "Anyhow, Ike went through here yesterday."

"I'm surprised you didn't have a dodger on him," I said.

He scowled, and sounded a little defensive when he spoke. "There was one. We found it just now, buried in a pile. Gave his name, but no picture, and a description that fit most anybody."

"I guess one like that wouldn't be of much use."

"Too bad, too," Storm said. "I'd have maybe got the publicity I need, had I known. People around here'd know then I wasn't over the hill."

"We'll be getting on," Frank said. "You think he headed north for Dolores?"

"Looked that way. Heading up into the San Miguels to hide maybe. Wish I could go with you, Frank. But I got to hold down the fort here."

They shook hands, and Frank said, "We have any luck, we'll stop here on the way out. Damned good to see you after all these years."

"My compliments to your beautiful wife," Storm said. He smiled at Lola. "Makes me wish I'd not stayed a bachelor."

Dolores was only ten or twelve miles up the rutted road. It looked like another cattle town mostly, although a set of narrow-gauge railroad tracks ran through it.

They came from Durango, which was about fifty miles east, and went up to the mining towns scattered through about a hundred miles of the San Miguels. That's what Jake Storm had told Frank.

Aside from that, the main difference was that it was smaller even than Cortez and had no substantial buildings. Here, everything was board-fronts.

We found a little cafe near the weathered depot, and went in to order coffee and try to get information from the proprietor.

He took our order, and while we waited I kept looking through the dirty front window at the depot sign. It read: DOLORES, COLORADO, RIO GRANDE SOUTHERN R.R., and for some reason I couldn't get it out of my mind.

The cafe man returned with the coffee and said, "You folks hear the news?"

"What news?" Lola said.

"About the robbery."

"What robbery?" I said.

"The train was robbed this morning. Just north of the town here. Holdup man took the mine payroll bound for Rico."

Ladd, who had been looking tired, was suddenly alert.

"Train robbed? Here?"

"Yep," the cafe man said. "First time in all the years the narrow-gauge has been running that it's ever been held up, far as I know."

"Who did it?" Frank said.

"Stranger passing through. Rode in on a pinto horse, yesterday, both of them looking wore out. Had a kind of Indian look, I thought. The man, I mean." He paused. "He saw that railroad sign and began asking questions about it and the amount of mining going on at places like Rico, forty miles up the line. I figured he was maybe looking for a job. He damned sure looked like he could use one. It had to be him that done it."

"And then?" Frank said.

"He paid for a meal and rode on out."

"And then?"

"Just after dawn comes the train in from Durango. Makes its regular stop, and pulls out. Twenty minutes later it comes backing down the tracks, and the engineer is yelling his head off and attracting a crowd. Said he'd stopped to clear some rocks looked like they'd fell off a cut up yonder. Then this stranger comes out of the brush, and throws down on him."

"He act like he knew what he was doing?" Frank said.

"Engineer said he sure as hell did. Made him open the express car, shot the lock off the strong box, emptied the contents into a canvas sack and rode off with it. Simple as that."

"How much did he get?"

"Payroll ain't too big nowadays at Rico. Production is off. Still, I heard he got a thousand dollars in currency."

"Fancy that," Frank said. He was eyeing first Lola, then me, and it was clear he was warning us to keep our mouths shut about Tolbert.

"What about the fireman, brakeman? Engineer wasn't alone," I said.

"I don't know. What I heard, I guess they was too surprised to be heroes. Wasn't none of them armed, it appears." He paused. "Been some conflict between the railroad and the mine owners about the rates charged lately, and I guess nobody was going to risk his life."

"Anybody get up a posse?" Frank said.

"Somebody telephoned Durango and they're sending the sheriff up. Expect him any time."

"How far?"

"How far where?"

"From Durango."

"About fifty miles."

"Take a long day to get here," Frank said.

"Hell, no!" the cafe man said. "The sheriff and his posse won't be riding horses. They're coming by cars."

"Railroad?"

"Where you been?" the cafe man said. "By cars, I mean auto cars."

"I was forgetting," Frank said.

"They'll be pulling into here anytime now. They'll get that bandit quick."

I think we all lost any appetite we had about then. We'd had a long hard chase after Tolbert, and a sheriff and his posse would cut us out of the reward.

"Durango is over in La Plata County," Frank said. "What's the sheriff from over there doing here?"

The cafe man shrugged. "That's the way it's been since we lost our own sheriff. That young Sheriff Wise is ambitious for a reputation. He sometimes bends the rules."

"Looks like it," Frank said. "Automobile posse!"

The cafe man nodded. "That ain't all," he said. "I understand they're going to send one of them aeroplanes over, too. To spot where he's hiding from the air."

"Aeroplane!" Frank scowled. "Goddamn! Where they going to get one of them?"

The cafe man walked over to his counter and came back with a cardboard poster. He laid it on the table in front of Frank.

I could just scan the caption before Frank grabbed it up. The caption read: BARNSTORMING AVIATOR BRINGS THRILLS TO DURANGO!

"What does it say?" Lola said.

"Some damned fool, one of them aviator fellas, has been all week showing off out of a pasture outside Durango."

"That young Sheriff Wise got in touch with him right off, is the rumor," the cafe man said. "That ought to be a sight to see! You ever see one of them things fly?"

"Don't care if I never do," Frank said.

"Man, you got to get with the times!"

I could see Frank bridle when he said that.

The cafe man went back to his kitchen, taking the poster with him.

Frank said slowly, "I recall that Ike said he still had it in for the railroads."

"He's fallen on hard times," I said. "From the Southern Pacific and the Santa Fe down to a narrow-gauge ore line."

"To him a railroad is a railroad, I guess," Frank said.

CHAPTER 18

THE sheriff from Durango and his heavily armed posse drove up just as we finished our coffee, paid our tab, and left the cafe.

They came roaring into the main dirt street, kicking up a hell of a dust, and scaring the life out of several hitchracked cow ponies.

Townsmen came pouring out of the board-fronts to greet them. We just stood on the portico in front of the cafe and stared.

When the dust settled, we were looking at a dozen men clambering out of a Dodge touring car and a couple of Fords.

The young one getting out of the driver's side of the Dodge was the only one wearing a badge.

The cafe man had come out just behind us and he said, "That's the sheriff. Sheriff Wise."

Frank said, "He as smart as his name sounds?"

"I told you that."

"So you did," Frank said. "But he didn't bring his aeroplane."

"It'll be along," the cafe man said.

Just then we could hear the drone of a gasoline engine coming out of the east.

"Could be it now."

We all turned and stared up at the eastern sky. The hum of the engine got closer.

There was still some dust in the air and it made it hard to see. A burst of engine blast dropped our gaze to another cloud of street dust, and there it was. Not an aeroplane at all—a motorcycle with a helmeted and goggled rider.

"What the hell do you call that?" Frank said.

"A motorcycle," the cafe man said.

"I mean the rider."

The rider dismounted, shoved his goggles up, and joined the rest of the posse.

"Poor Ike," Lola said. "They sent an army to do a man's job."

Frank made no comment on that. He just kept staring at all those men. But he had a faint scowl and a thoughtful look.

When he spoke, he said, "It ain't right."

"What?" the cafe man asked.

"That sheriff. Wise. He's got no business being here. What about the deputy at Cortez?"

"I don't know. Whoever called, called Wise. Lately, it's just like I said, we been doing that. Anything big, Wise has been taking over," the cafe man said. "We like him better anyhow. He's got up-to-date ways of doing things."

"I can see that," Frank said, and there was an edge to his voice. "Puts me in mind some of Ardmore."

"Who?"

"A man we left behind us. You wouldn't know him."

"Well, Frank?" Lola said.

"Let's watch and see what they do."

The cafe man crossed the street to join a group of townspeople around the sheriff, who was gesturing and asking questions.

Wise was a lean, tough-looking young guy who, from where we stood, did remind me of Ardmore. Except he had darker eyes.

Something about his manner seemed so much like Buck's that it gave you an eerie feeling, kind of like you were seeing Buck brought back from the dead. Two of a kind, was my impression. Like twins.

"Don't let him know we're after Ike," Frank said.

"You still have hope?" I said.

"We came this far," he said. "We can't give up without a try." He moved across the street and we followed.

Wise even sounded like Ardmore talking.

We couldn't get close because of the crowd around him, but he had a strong, authoritative voice that carried to the fringe where we were.

By then he'd got all the information about the robbery that any of the locals could give him. He took one of them, who seemed knowledgeable, by the sleeve and led him over to the Dodge and motioned him onto the front seat.

The others all climbed back into their vehicles, except for one whose seat was now taken by the local guide. This one stood on the running board, holding onto the framework of the top. The sheriff got behind the steering wheel and led the procession north out of town along the dirt road that paralleled the tracks of the Rio Grande Southern.

The Fords fell in behind, and bringing up the drag was the goggled motorcycle rider.

"Going up to the site of the crime," Frank said. "Mount up! We don't want to lose them."

We followed the motorcycle, but it was soon out of sight.

"Damned things go fast, don't they?" Frank said.

Neither Lola or I answered him. I think we both had in mind that we'd lost the game.

A lot of the townspeople came right along with us.

It was only a couple of miles to where Ike had stopped the train. As we closed in we could see the posse out of their vehicles and standing around a cluster of boulders that had been removed from the rails.

Two of the posse had walked off to the east and were studying a faint road leading into some round, sage-covered hills. They were dressed in range clothes, but there was something that put me in mind of the Ute that Frank had shot by mistake. When we got closer they looked even more like him.

"Utes?" I said.

He nodded. "If so, they'll pick up his trail in a hurry."

"Would he use the road?"

"He might, at the start. He'd be in a hurry to get away. Once back in there, I reckon he'd branch off."

"I wonder if they know who he is?"

"Mingle in there with that bunch, Drew. See if you can find out."

I left my horse with him and Lola, and worked my way in close to the sheriff. "Anybody know who it was that did it?" I said.

The sheriff's eyes swung to me, and for a minute I thought I'd made a mistake in asking. But then he seemed to write me off as just another curious onlooker, and turned back to a conversation he was having with one of the posse.

Somebody else said, "Sure we know. Was some unknown saddle-bum that come through town and asked about the train schedule." He paused. "Seen a way to make hisself a quick grubstake, I reckon. It's a funny thing, but all the year's the Southern's been running, since back in '91, I never heard of it being robbed. Took some grubliner to think of it. Ain't that a kick?"

"Ironical as hell," I said. And after a few minutes I wandered back to Frank and told him what the local had said.

"Good!" he said. "What they don't know won't hurt us."

I didn't know what he meant by that exactly, but I did know then that he wasn't going to give up the chase.

I thought of something then. "If that sheriff recognizes you, he's going to get curious what you're doing up here."

"He won't know me," Frank said. "Not a kid his age."

"He's older than I am."

"That's different, Drew. You being interested in the old days. It ain't likely he shares your interest."

"Let's hope so," I said. It was something to worry about, though.

But the real worry now was how to make our next move. If we started up that road the Utes were scouting, we were sure to arouse the objections of the sheriff. He'd not chance any trail sign being obliterated. Besides, he'd want to know what business we had there in the first place.

So we had to wait until the sheriff and his men made their own move.

It wasn't long in coming.

They suddenly all got back into the Dodge and the Fords, holding their assortment of weapons, leaving behind them this time the townsman who'd led them to the holdup site. And they went roaring up the slight grade, spewing dust and gravel behind them.

The man on the motorcycle followed.

"All right," Frank said. "We'll stay behind them, so's not to attract attention."

"Won't be hard to do," I said. "They must have been going twenty-five miles an hour when they left."

"They may get slowed down up ahead," he said. "We'll keep an eye open for that."

Lola said, "You'll have some explaining to do if we blunder into them."

"We'll try to avoid that," Frank said.

I was wondering what his intentions were, if any. It seemed to me that he could have nothing planned, was just plodding along because we'd been doing so for so long that it'd become a habit. Maybe he was hoping for something to break in our favor, but I couldn't think of what it would be.

As far as I was concerned, we were licked. I found myself cussing out Tolbert for robbing the train, and thus bringing in the sheriff's posse to ruin our chances.

Really though, catching Tolbert now didn't mean much to me. I wasn't going to share in the reward. A hundred dollars in wages was the only difference to me one way or the other.

To be honest, I knew my own goal wasn't to get Ike, it was to get Lola.

There it was. Being around her day and night, there was hardly anytime she wasn't in my mind. Having once satisfied it, my lust for her was almost unbearable now.

A lot of my admiration for Frank remained, but some of it had been lost along the trail. He had made some mistakes in judgment that had had their effects.

But mostly it was because I wanted Lola so badly that I was looking deliberately for faults in Frank. I guess so I wouldn't feel guilty for the way I felt about her.

It was tough, lusting after the wife of the man who'd been my idol.

CHAPTER 19

THE vehicles had barely disappeared into the hills when we heard the roar of another engine.

It was Lola who looked up and said, "My God! The aeroplane!"

And there it was. It came laboring along, a couple of hundred feet above the train tracks. It headed almost for us, it seemed, before the pilot cut his engine, veered slightly, and glided toward a flat, grassy meadow nearby.

"Seemed damned eager to get down," Frank said.

He kept staring as the pilot gunned his engine, blasted the craft around, and came taxiing over the pasture to where we and the townsfolks were standing.

When he reached us, he stopped the engine and climbed out of the rear open cockpit. He was wearing a tight-fitting leather helmet and cavalry boots, similar to those of the motorcycle rider. He had his goggles pushed up on his forehead, and a long white silk scarf looped around his neck with the end flung over his shoulder. He was bundled into a heavy sheepskin jacket and looked to be about thirty years old.

He was conscious of being the center of attention, and he stepped down from the side of the plane with his head held high in profile. That was a mistake because he put one of his boots right into a green cow pad.

He glanced down, then brought his head up again and pretended not to notice.

"Anybody seen the sheriff?" he said.

Somebody pointed to the trail just as the posse's vehicles came roaring back. "Must have seen you coming."

I'd seen a plane somewhat similar to this one last year in Prescott. I couldn't remember what it was called, and I asked the pilot.

"Curtiss biplane," he said proudly. "Got a ninety horse-power engine."

I was looking at the JN-2 painted on the fabric side. "Called a Jenny, isn't it?" I asked. "On account of the letters there."

"That's right," he said. He was watching now the approach of the Dodge driven by the sheriff.

The sheriff drew up, got out, and shook the pilot's hand. "Sheriff Wise," he said. "You're Rockenbach, the one I talked to this morning by telephone?"

The pilot nodded. "What do you want me to do, Sheriff?"

"Can you fly that thing back into those hills?"

Rockenbach looked. "The hills, yeah. But the mountains, they're something else. The air's too thin for me to go up there. We're near a mile high here at ground level."

"What I want you to do is fly back in there and try to spot a saddle-tramp on a pinto horse. We'll go in as far as the road goes. If you see him, come back and waggle your wings over us and lead us to him."

"Will do," the pilot said. "All I need is a couple of men to hold my wing tips while I give that propeller a twist."

Two of the posse did so.

The pilot went to the plane and leaned into the cockpit and fiddled with a switch. He went forward then to the nose of the plane and pulled the propeller through a few times. He gave it a sudden, fast snap and the engine caught, and he ran to the cockpit and climbed in. He signaled the wing holders to let go, and the plane began to creep across the meadow.

For a few minutes you couldn't hear anything except gasoline engines, and then they were all on their way, roaring back into the hills.

In search of one half-breed Navajo on a worn-out pinto pony.

CHAPTER 20

BECAUSE he was in a hurry, most likely was the reason Tolbert had stuck to the road in the beginning. Of course he'd had no way of knowing he'd be chased by vehicles. Having been locked away all those years, the thought probably had never entered his head.

It made it easy for the posse. All they had to do was keep the two Ute trackers hanging on the running boards, watching for where Ike might have turned off. For that reason they went slower than they might have, not wanting to miss anything.

Still, they went faster than Ike could have gone, and we guessed they'd be gaining on him, because they were leaving us further behind all the time.

The tire tracks were plain in the road—it wasn't much more than a trail now, looking like it hadn't been used for a long time. Possibly, we thought, it led to some abandoned ranch or something back there in the hills.

The aeroplane, though, had long since disappeared from our sight.

With all that engine noise behind him, it wouldn't be very long before Tolbert knew something was coming, even if he didn't know what the hell it was.

He'd no doubt seen automobiles now and then since his release from the lockup. And he might have seen a motorcycle or two. But an aeroplane must have been a startling sight to him, although he could have been aware they existed, even in prison.

Suddenly some of the noise up ahead of us stopped. We

rode on a little way, and then we almost skylined ourselves at the brow of a hill before we were stopped by Frank's warning.

There, a mile or so away beyond a shallow valley, we saw where the road ended at an abandoned mine in the side of another hill. The automobiles were parked there, and the members of the posse were standing around while the Utes scouted the area.

"Road's end," Frank said.

Just then we heard the aeroplane chugging away, and the pilot flew over sheriff's men and wagged his wings. He circled around and made a landing on the road and rolled to a bumpy halt.

There was a big discussion then as the sheriff and the others came rushing to him. We could see him pointing and gesticulating and the sheriff waving his arms in return.

The pilot crawled over the side and stood to relieve himself. Then he went to the nose as two of the posse turned the plane around and held the wings. He got the propeller turning, got back into the cockpit, gunned his engine, and roared into a takeoff.

He just cleared the hill behind the old mine.

He circled and flew off in the direction from which he'd come a few minutes before, and we could see the posse members taking canteens and weapons out of the vehicles and moving out on foot toward the south.

"Let's go!" Frank said.

"Where?" I said.

"He waggled his wings, didn't he? That was the signal he was to give if he spotted Ike."

"So?"

"They're on foot and we're riding," Frank said. "We'll head the direction that flying machine went and hope to get to where Ike is before they do."

We dropped back into a draw behind our hill and mounted up. We were lucky there, because the draw led to a long wash that kept going in roughly the right direction. We hoped it continued. If so, we could pick up a quick lead on the walking posse.

Every now and then the aeroplane would come flying back into sight, then turn to go off again, waggling its wings.

I guess the aviator had his hands full flying the thing and looking down at the posse, because he didn't seem to see us in the wash. We could tell as he flew past us each time that we were pulling ahead of the sheriff's men. Frank was pushing the horses.

There came a time when we could see the plane circling around and around a short ways ahead.

We climbed up the side of the wash and we saw then what the pilot was circling. As we'd suspected, it was Ike and his pinto.

As we watched we saw Ike dismount, pull a rifle from its scabbard, take aim upward, and fire.

At that time the aeroplane couldn't have been more than a couple of hundred feet above him, and he could hardly miss.

He must have at least punctured a hole in the fabric, because the pilot banked away in a hurry and began flying at a radius of three or four hundred yards. If nothing else it put a hell of a scare into him, I'd bet.

We saw Ike remount and continue riding southward.

"He isn't much of a rifleman," Lola said.

"It's like I said, what do you expect after twenty years of no practice," Frank said.

"I was forgetting," she said. "All those years. No wonder he'd rather die than be locked up again."

Frank said, "He didn't see us."

"The aviator?" I asked.

"Neither of them, I think. If we can keep ahead of those men on foot we'll try to take Ike and run."

"Where to?"

"Back to Cortez. We're going that direction."

One good thing, Tolbert kept riding south. The bad thing

was that the aeroplane kept flying around in that wide circle, out of range of his rifle, and keeping him in sight.

As it came around on the next pass it flew right over our heads and I saw the surprised look on the pilot's face as he saw us.

Frank noticed that too, because he jerked out his carbine and fired a shot at it as it pulled away. He didn't appear to hit anything.

He said, "Damn my eyes!" and shoved the weapon back into its boot.

"Did you want to hit the pilot, Frank?" Lola said.

He gave her a quick look, and shook his head. "God, no! That'd be murder. I was trying to knock him down."

"That could be murder, too," I said. "If he crashed."

Lola was staring at the long, flat, near-brushless bottom of the wash. She said, "Drew, can those things fly without power?"

I thought back to the landings the pilot had made to confer with the sheriff and said, "He always cuts the engine to land, then glides in."

She didn't say another word, just pulled out her Winchester and levered in a cartridge.

We watched the plane, and sure enough here he came again, only now he was flying farther out from us.

"Damn!" I said.

Lola didn't say a word. She just tracked the plane as it circled around to the west of us. We could barely make out the pilot's head above the cockpit.

"Goddammit, Lola, don't shoot him!" Frank said.

My mouth dry, not knowing exactly what she'd do.

She waited until he was even with us, fired one round, and shattered the propeller. The engine revved up instantly.

The pilot cut it quick and went into a powerless glide toward the bed of the arroyo.

Lola had already put her carbine away. Just like that. Little Sure Shot again, I thought.

We kept riding along behind the plane as it glided lower and lower in the distance. It must have gone a quarter mile down the draw before its wheels touched down. It rolled only a short way in the dry sand, then came to an abrupt stop as the tail flipped up and the nose dug in.

We gigged the horses and got up to it just as the pilot got out, looking kind of dazed. There was a small cut on his face where he'd slammed it against the dash or something. He focused on us and began to swear.

"What the hell did you do that for?" he said.

"Never did like insects buzzing around my head," Frank said. He looked at the aeroplane. "Don't seem like your flying machine is damaged much."

"How am I going to get it out of here without a propeller?"

"There's enough of your friends back there to hand-carry it out," Frank said.

The pilot scowled viciously. "My friends happen to be the sheriff and his posse," he said. "You're in big trouble, mister."

Frank looked him over, saw he had no gun. "Maybe so. But not right away, I reckon."

"You owe me for a new propeller," the aviator said.

"Present a bill to the sheriff," Frank said. "If you start walking north you'll reach him in an hour if you don't get lost."

"What the hell are you doing out here anyway?" the pilot said. He looked at us more closely. "Hey! I saw you this morning where they assembled the search party!"

"We're the original search party," Frank said.

The pilot stared. "So that's it! You're racing the sheriff for the reward!"

"What reward?"

"The Rio Grande Southern has put five hundred dollars on his head." The pilot stopped short after he said that. He had the sudden look of a man who wished he'd bitten off his tongue before he spoke.

Frank swung back into his saddle, kicked his mount, and started off with us behind him.

"Hey!" the aviator said. "What about me?"

"Better get to walking," Frank said. "You got a ways to go."

We rode away then, leaving him standing there. When I looked back a few minutes later, he was trudging northward, kicking up sand as if he was mad.

"He could make trouble for you, Frank," I said. "This isn't the old days."

"Hell, I know that," he said. "About the old days, I mean. That flying contraption back there is proof of that."

Now we could no longer simply follow along the wash, letting the plane guide us on Tolbert's trail. I wondered if he could have heard Frank's and Lola's shots over the drone of the aeroplane engine. I doubted it.

We climbed up out of the wash to study the place we'd last seen Tolbert, but he had disappeared, gone probably into the rolling country beyond.

We could spend time looking for his trail sign, or we could try to guess his route by the contour of the terrain.

We didn't have the time to waste.

We were all thinking the same thing. There was damned little chance the pilot would prevail on the posse to haul his plane out. Not at this time.

What the posse would do is hightail it back to their vehicles, backtrack to the Rio Grande Southern rails and the road into Dolores. They'd hope to cut us off as we came out of the hills southeast of the town.

How far south depended on when we got out and when, or if, the pilot intercepted the sheriff's bunch. There was always the hope he might roam around half-lost and miss them. It was more likely he wouldn't; he'd been flying above the terrain and would know their approximate location.

We kept riding along, but we didn't see Ike and that pinto again. I could see Frank looking worried.

I said, "You think he might have turned back somewhere?"

"Why would he?" Frank said. "I think the poor bastard just don't know what to do. This is the first time he's ever been chased by automobiles and aeroplanes, for cripe's sake!'

"What would you do if you were him?" I said.

"That's just it," he said. "I wouldn't know what to do either. It ain't fair, goddammit!"

We saw him then, just as we came up to what later proved to be the last range of hills. He'd stopped, and we could see him up on the brow of one of them, and he appeared to be studying the lay of the land ahead.

We dismounted in the screening of some brush.

"How're we going to take him?" I said.

Even as I spoke, Tolbert moved to his horse and got up in his saddle.

I heard Lola move beside me, and she had her rifle in her hands.

"Shoot the horse!" Frank said.

She fired, and blood spurted back of the pinto's right ear. It went down, forelegs folding first, then its body toppled sideways.

Tolbert tried to leap free, but his left foot caught in a stirrup. He didn't get his leg quite clear. It looked like the dead weight of the pinto pinned his ankle to the ground.

We rode fast toward him.

His back was toward us, but I could see he was wearing a gun and holster and his right hand was free. I could still feel the wound of that gun, from back in the bat cave.

"Watch that handgun!" I said.

"I'm watching," Frank said.

He was pinned facing away from us, but he heard us and grabbed the pistol and pulled it loose. He tried to twist his body enough to see us, but he couldn't quite make it.

"Who's back there?" he said.

Frank drew his own gun as he walked toward him. "Frank Ladd," he said.

"Frank!"

"Yeah."

"Frank, get this goddamn horse off my leg!"

Frank slipped up behind him, grabbed his wrist and jerked the gun out of his hand. "Sure, Ike."

"I think it's broke."

"We'll see."

Frank and I and Lola too, got around where we could lift the horse's weight just enough so he could pull his ankle free. We could hear him groan.

"Sweet Jesus!" he said.

That must have been something he learned a long time ago in a missionary school, I thought.

There was a sack tied to his saddle horn.

"That the train money?" Frank said.

"Take it, Frank, and help me get away. Take it instead of the bounty." He groaned again, as if struck by sharp pain.

"Let me see that leg," Frank said. He took the boot in his hands and began to draw it off slowly.

Tolbert gritted his teeth and sweat broke out all over his face, but he didn't cry out. Frank felt the shinbone and the ankle joint. He looked more like a doctor then than he did a manhunter.

"Ike," he said, "I don't think there's any bones broke."

"Put the boot back on then," Tolbert said. "Do it while you still can."

Frank thought it over for a minute, then he forced the boot back on over the swelling tissues. The sweat burst heavier out of Tolbert's brow. He groaned this time. "Goddammit!" he said. "It might be best if you shoot me."

"I don't have to, if it ain't broke," Frank said.

I guess he meant it to be a joke. He turned to me then, and said, "Drew, Ike will ride your horse. You'll ride Lola's, and she'll ride double on behind."

I didn't object. I went to her mount and began lengthening the stirrups. She met my eyes, but I couldn't read hers.

Frank took my carbine off my horse and stuck it behind

his own scabbard. He tied Tolbert's hands to the saddle horn, after helping him get his injured foot into the stirrup. He put a lead rope on the mount and tied it to his own saddle.

With Lola clinging to me on her horse, and Frank leading Tolbert on mine, we moved out from the hills and almost at once we saw the rail line east from Dolores toward Durango. There was a road beside it.

We pulled up to make sure the road was empty.

Frank said, "That posse will take some time to get back to their vehicles and drive around. I hope we got time to find a road south to Cortez."

He turned west toward Dolores, and found a branch road almost at once. There was a wood sign there shaped like an arrow with the name painted on it that said, *Cortez, 10 miles.*

We started down the road, and what it came down to now was could we reach Cortez and that deputy friend of Frank's before the Durango sheriff and his men in those damned automobiles came around and overtook us.

"Maybe we ought to get off the road," I said. "Get off where they can't use the vehicles."

"Wouldn't do us no good," Frank said. "They'd get to Cortez ahead of us then. And there ain't no other place around we could turn Ike in."

"It's a damned big gamble."

"It's our best chance."

"That Durango sheriff could legally accept Ike, and give us credit for the capture."

"You think he would? Don't be a damned fool, Drew. The best that glory hunter would do is say we had joined his posse, and the most we'd get would be maybe one share split among a dozen men. If any. He's out for a reputation, Drew, and he'd hog all the credit even if it meant lying to get it."

"You sure?"

"Sure enough not to gamble on it. In my mind he's another Ardmore. Would you trust *him*?

That clinched it, as far as I was concerned.

Tolbert had been listening to all this, but not saying a word. And his face showed no expression. I wondered what he was thinking.

We had covered probably half the distance to Cortez before I turned and saw the dust behind us and the three automobiles and the motorcycle kicking it up. They'd just come over the brow above a dip in the dirt roadway about a mile back.

I yelled, "They're there!" And right then we went down into another road dip.

Lola said, "Keep hidden, Frank. All of you!" She reached around me and slid her rifle out of its boot and dropped off the horse, almost sprawling as she hit the ground. It was lucky we weren't trotting. I reined up and jerked around to look at her. Frank had stopped too, and I saw her exchange stares with him. Then she stepped up to the crest of the slope we'd just descended.

"Stay out of sight," she said and slid to a prone position.

I dropped the reins and crawled up beside her. I could see the vehicles coming fast, not more than a quarter mile away now. Lola watched until they drew to half of that.

Her Winchester cracked twice and the lead car, which was the Dodge, swerved, straightened, then halted after grinding a few feet on flattened tires.

The Ford behind ran into the Dodge, and the second Ford ran into the first, and we could hear the sounds of the collisions.

Her Winchester kept cracking away as she shot out more tires. I was struck by her coolness. It was like such shooting was all in a day's work for her.

The posse had scattered into the brush.

We remounted, and Frank said to her, "You think they can keep coming?"

She nodded. "But slow. Those flat tires won't roll well on a rocky dirt road. And I drilled the radiator of the one in the lead.

CHAPTER 21

AS we rode into Cortez there were a few people on the street. But nobody seemed much interested in us, even though if they'd looked close they'd have noticed Tolbert's mount being led and that his hands were lashed to the horn over which the reins were looped.

We pulled up in front of the law office. Frank dismounted, dropping the lead rope.

Jake Storm came out to see us. He wasn't wearing a gun, and his eyes looked tired, like he'd been doing some unwelcome desk work. "What you got here?" he asked Frank.

"Tolbert," Frank said. "You got a vacant cell?"

"They're all vacant," Storm said.

I'd got down and was walking toward Frank to help him get Tolbert down.

Tolbert said it loud and clear, "I can't stand no more cells, Frank!"

"Get it open, Jake," Frank said to Storm.

"Sure thing," Storm said and turned toward the door.

Frank untied Tolbert's hands.

"No cell!" Tolbert yelled. He kicked the horse, and had a grasp now on the reins.

The horse knocked Frank off balance, and he stumbled backward and fell.

I reached for my Smith & Wesson, and hesitated. Maybe I was afraid of killing my horse. Maybe it was something else.

Tolbert turned the mount into a narrow throughway between the law office and the building next to it.

Frank was on his feet, cussing. He grabbed his carbine

from his saddle and collided with me as we both tried to enter the narrow pass-through.

He outweighed me, and he shoved me aside and went on, just as Lola came running into me from behind. I felt her Winchester slap against me as she squeezed by. Then I was running after her.

We all reached the rear of the building just as Tolbert drove the mount into the fringe of the brush beyond.

Frank raised his carbine and fired and missed.

I shot my handgun, knowing he was beyond effective range.

There was one more glimpse of Tolbert, high on the horse above the brush and receding fast, two hundred yards away.

I heard the crack then of Lola's weapon.

Tolbert fell out of the saddle and disappeared.

Jake Storm came running up. "What's going on?"

Frank and Lola exchanged glances. She said, "He made a break for it. We all shot at him."

"And he got away!"

"No," Lola said. "You'll find his body out there. Dead."

Storm said, "Dead, ma'am? How can you be so sure?"

"Because Frank Ladd never misses," she said, staring into the deputy's eyes.

EPILOGUE

WELL, there wasn't any real protest about who should get the reward money, although it took several weeks to go through the channels of authority, which I guess is usual routine.

The sheriff from Durango tried to protest at first, but Jake Storm backed up Frank all the way.

Wise then tried to put in a claim for ruined tires and a radiator, but Frank swore it wasn't him that did it, and there weren't any witnesses to prove who did.

Frank did pay for a new propeller for that aviator, who sent him a bill eventually after he found out who Frank Ladd was.

That wasn't hard to do if you were reading the newspapers anywhere in the West. And in some of those in the East too, I understand.

Frank Ladd was a legend again.

The Staffold council offered him the marshal's job at an increased salary, just to bring fame to the town. None of them ever knew why Buck Ardmore never came back. It was just as if he'd disappeared from the face of the earth.

I eventually heard that Frank and Lola bought a nice bungalow with part of the reward.

When I left, they hadn't yet done that, but they both shook my hand and wished me luck.

What did I get out of it?

Experience, that's about all.

I learned there can be more behind a living legend than meets the eye.

And I learned that a man can never completely understand a woman.

After I left, I never saw her again. She wanted it that way, she said.

I kept some copies of the news stories that heralded Frank's capture of Tolbert, and I used to read them now and then, and it always excited me to know I'd been along when it happened.

One that I'll always remember carried a dateline of Tucson, August, 1915:

WESTERN LEGEND FRANK LADD RIDES AGAIN!

Old-time lawman repeats capture of vicious badman! Frank Ladd last week ended the crime spree of the ex-convict killer, Ike Tolbert. He did it with a single rifle shot that proved he is still the great gunfighter he was in yesteryear . . .

It thrilled me to read it, even though I knew it was mostly myth.

If you have enjoyed this book and would like to receive details of other Walker Western titles, please write to:

Western Editor
Walker and Company
720 Fifth Avenue
New York, NY 10019